W9-BCP-663

THE SEVEN VOYAGES OF SINBAD

STONE ARCH BOOKS
a capstone imprint

THE SEVEN VOYAGES OF SINBAD

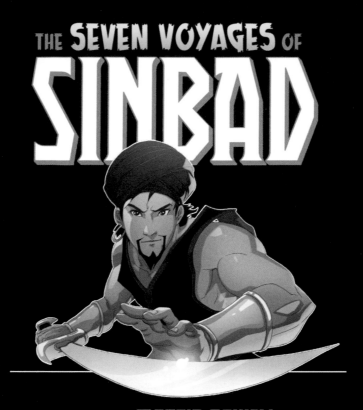

RETOLD BY **MARTIN POWELL**
ILLUSTRATED BY **FERRAN**

DESIGNER: **BRANN GARVEY**
EDITOR: **DONALD LEMKE**
ASSOC. EDITOR: **SEAN TULIEN**

ART DIRECTOR: **BOB LENTZ**
CREATIVE DIRECTOR: **HEATHER KINDSETH**
EDITORIAL DIRECTOR: **MICHAEL DAHL**

Published by Stone Arch Books in 2011 A Capstone Imprint 151 Good Counsel Drive, P.O. Box 669
Mankato, Minnesota 56002 www.capstonepub.com All rights reserved. No part of this publication may
be reproduced in whole or in part, or stored in a retrieval system, or transmitted in any form or by any
means, electronic, mechanical, photocopying, recording, or otherwise, without written permission.

Cataloging-in-Publication Data is available on the Library of Congress website.

ISBN: 978-1-4342-1987-9 (library binding)
ISBN: 978-1-4342-2775-1 (paperback)

Summary: The tale of Sinbad the Sailor, who goes to sea in search of great riches and discovers even
greater adventures. On his seven treacherous voyages, the Persian explorer braves a shipwreck, fights off
savage cannibals, and battles a giant Cyclops, hoping to survive and tell his legendary story.

Printed in the United States of America in Stevens Point, Wisconsin.
042010
005741WZF10

CONTENTS

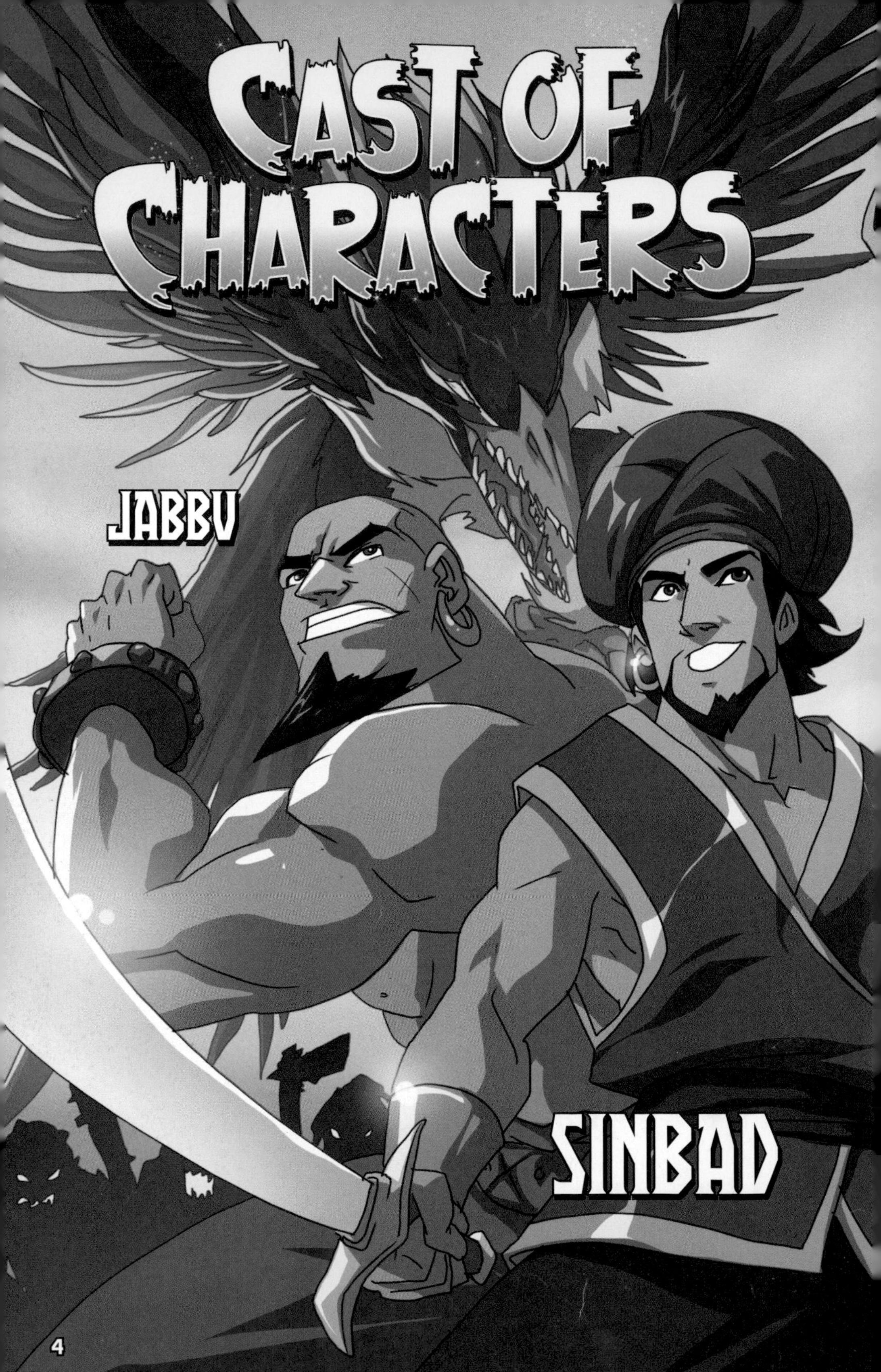
CAST OF CHARACTERS
JABBU
SINBAD

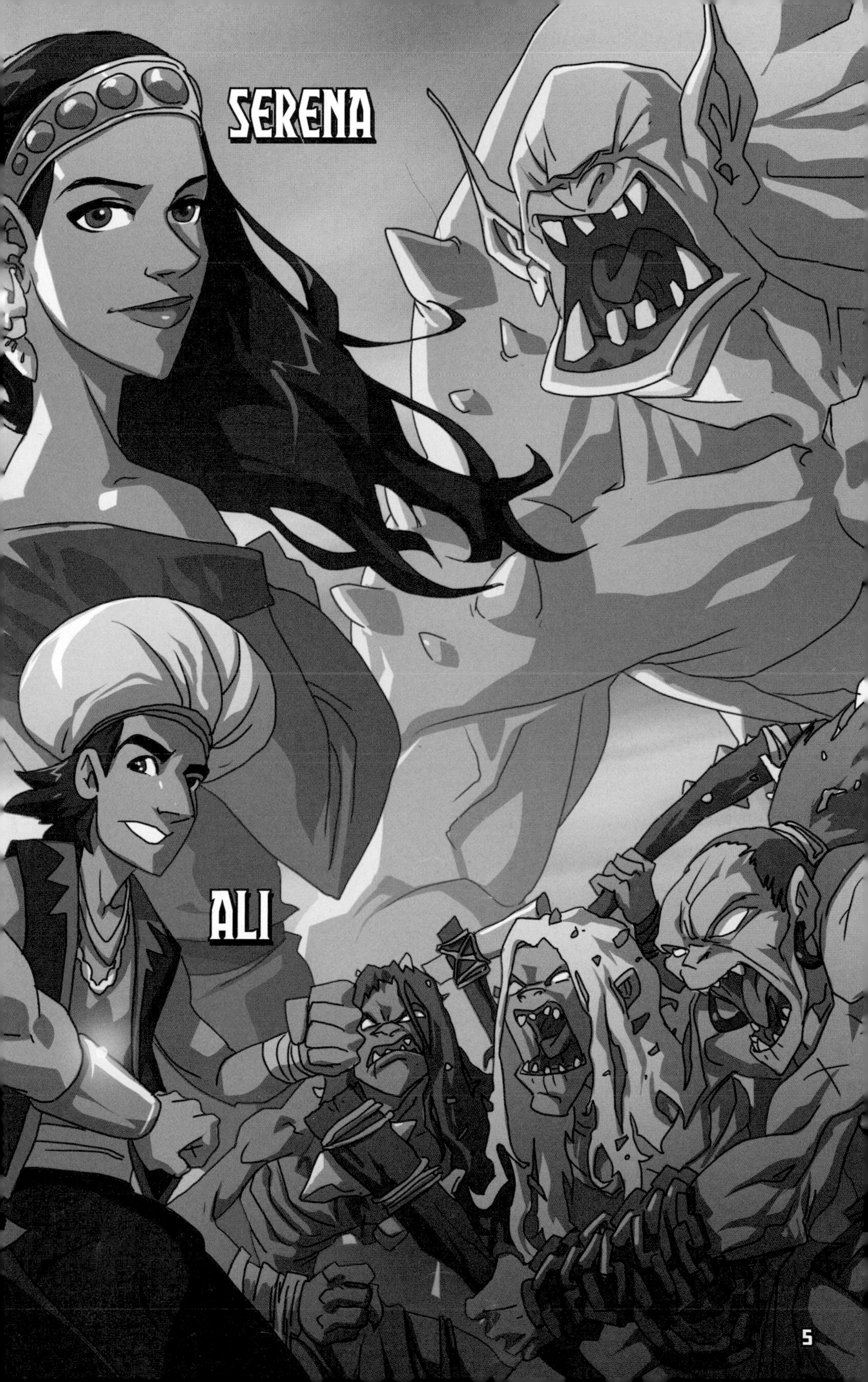
SERENA
ALI

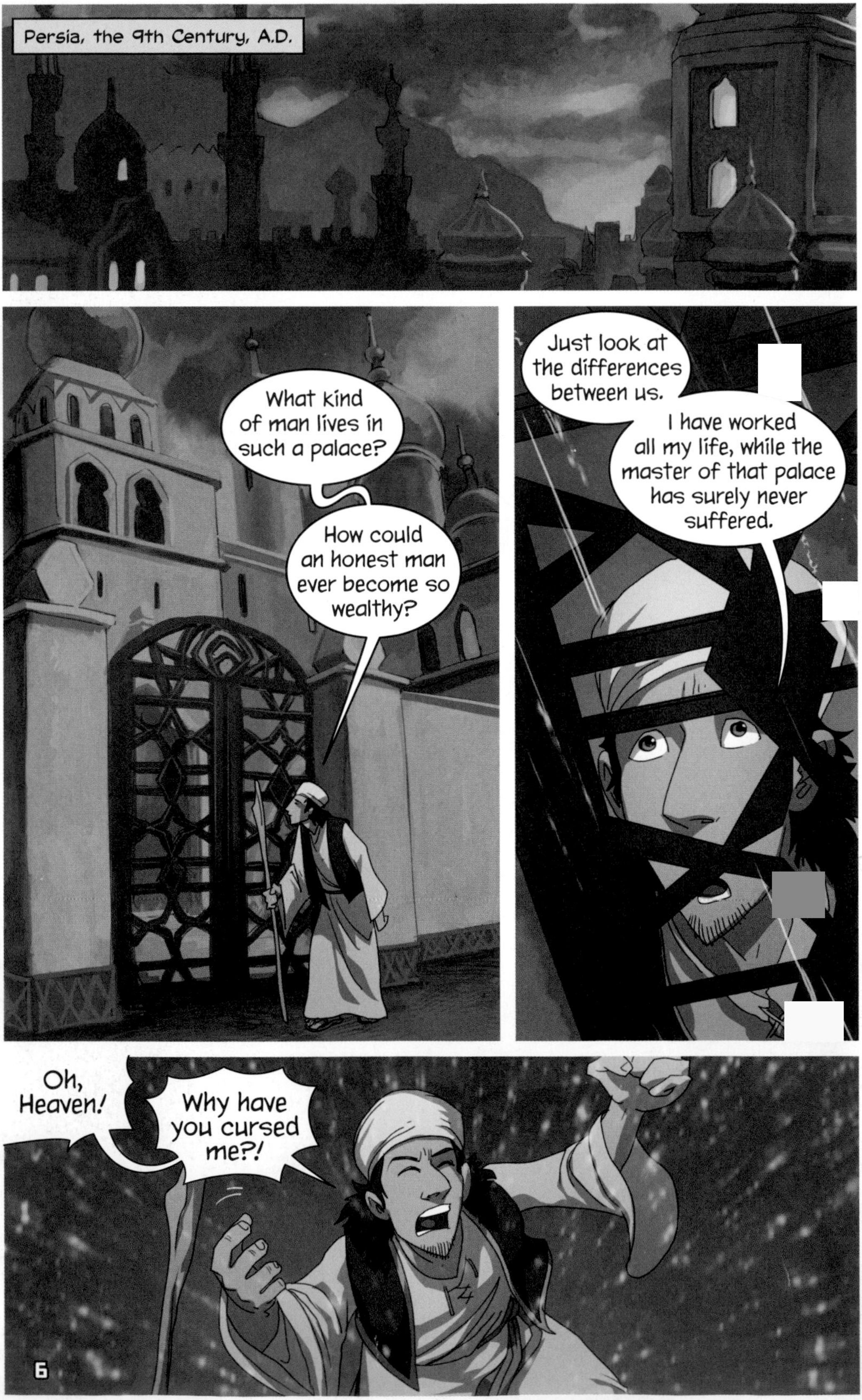
Persia, the 9th Century, A.D.
What kind of man lives in such a palace?
How could an honest man ever become so wealthy?
Just look at the differences between us.
I have worked all my life, while the master of that palace has surely never suffered.
Oh, Heaven!
Why have you cursed me?!

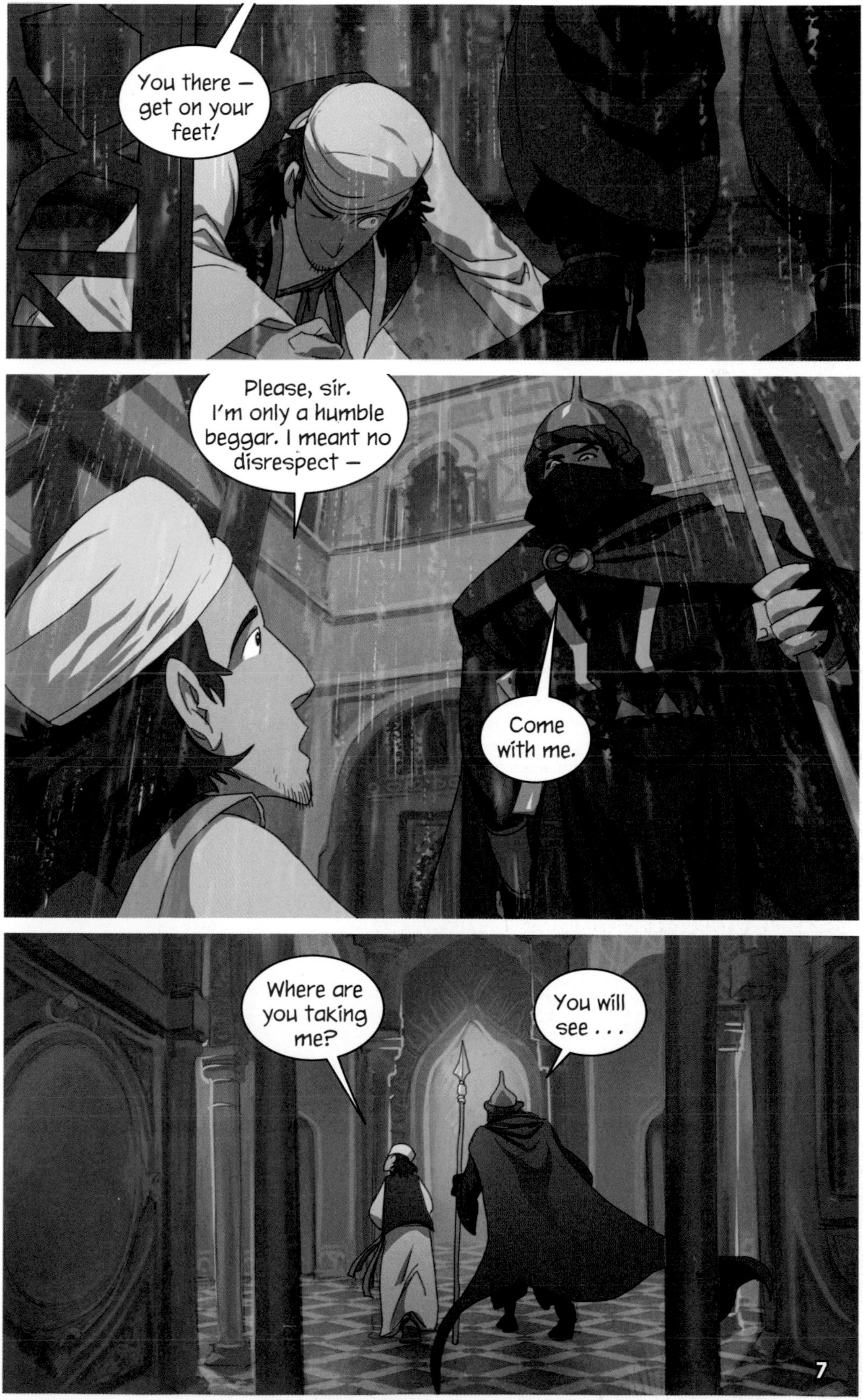
You there — get on your feet!
Please, sir. I'm only a humble beggar. I meant no disrespect —
Come with me.
Where are you taking me?
You will see . . .

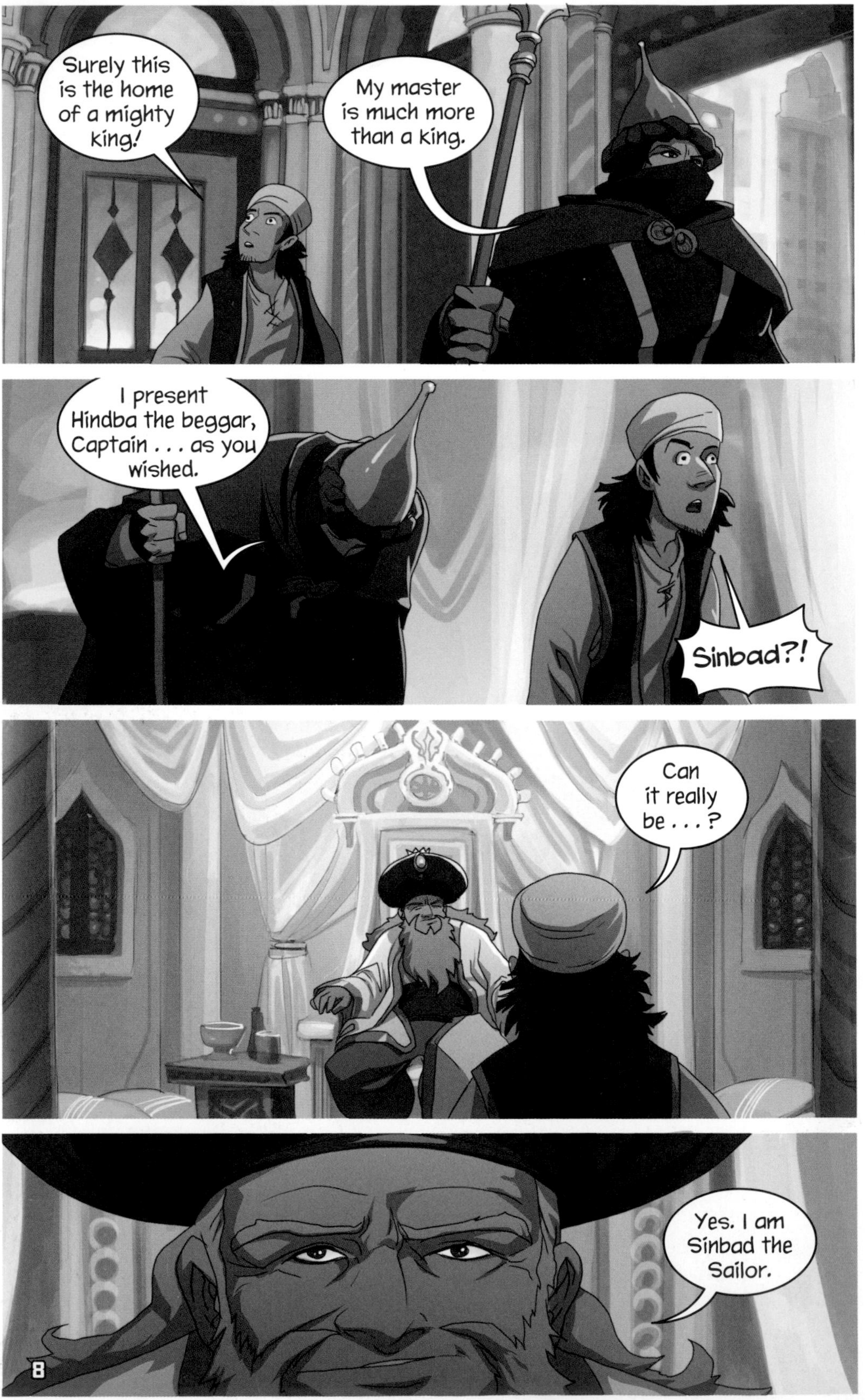
Surely this is the home of a mighty king!
My master is much more than a king.
I present Hindba the beggar, Captain . . . as you wished.
Sinbad?!
Can it really be . . . ?
Yes. I am Sinbad the Sailor.

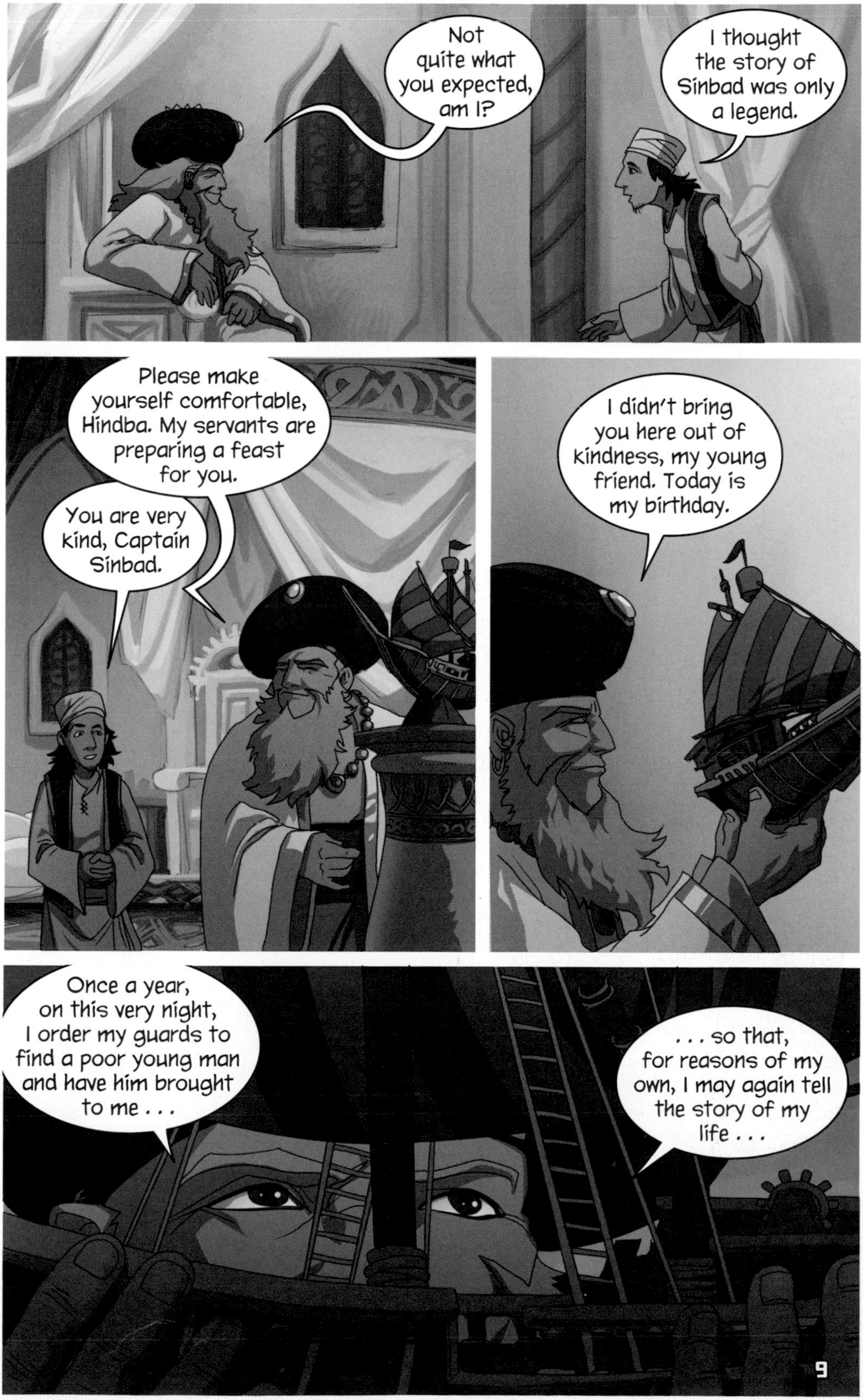
Not quite what you expected, am I?
I thought the story of Sinbad was only a legend.
Please make yourself comfortable, Hindba. My servants are preparing a feast for you.
You are very kind, Captain Sinbad.
I didn't bring you here out of kindness, my young friend. Today is my birthday.
Once a year, on this very night, I order my guards to find a poor young man and have him brought to me . . .
. . . so that, for reasons of my own, I may again tell the story of my life . . .

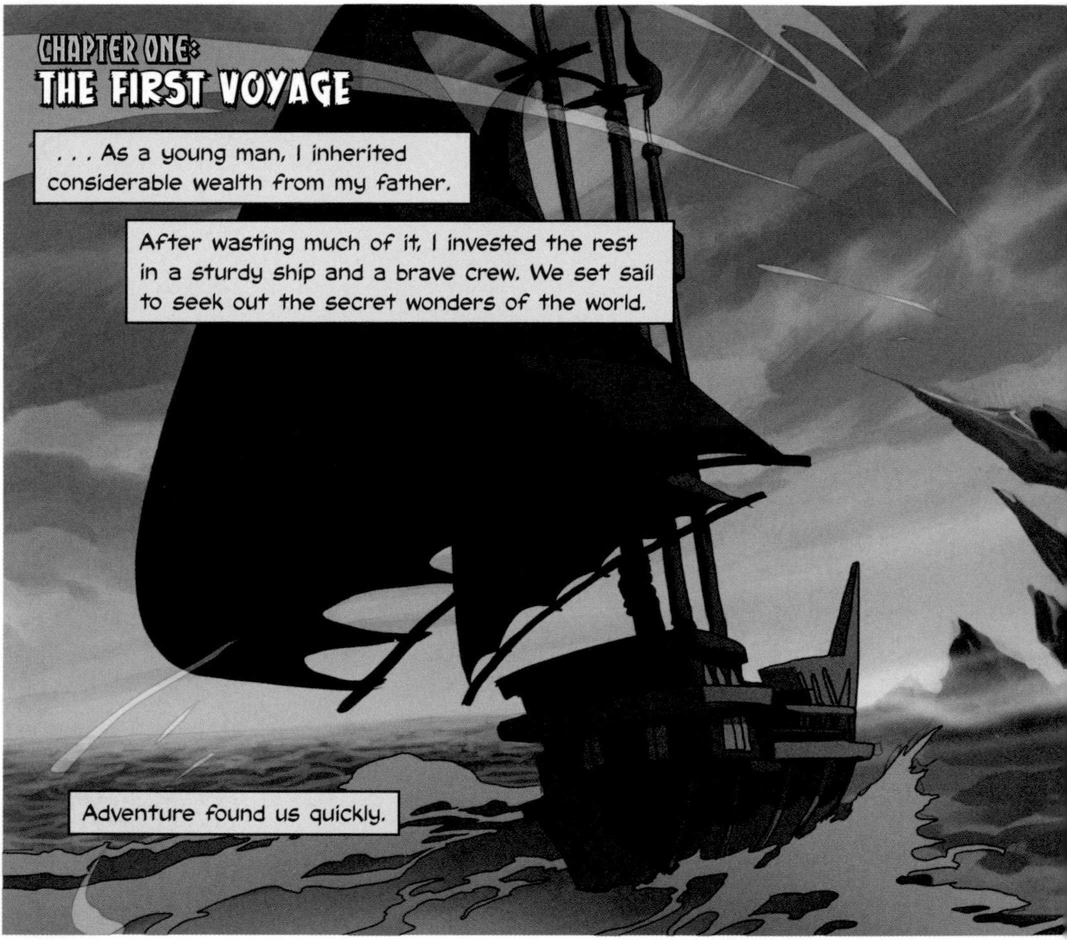
CHAPTER ONE:
THE FIRST VOYAGE
. . . As a young man, I inherited considerable wealth from my father.
After wasting much of it, I invested the rest in a sturdy ship and a brave crew. We set sail to seek out the secret wonders of the world.
Adventure found us quickly.

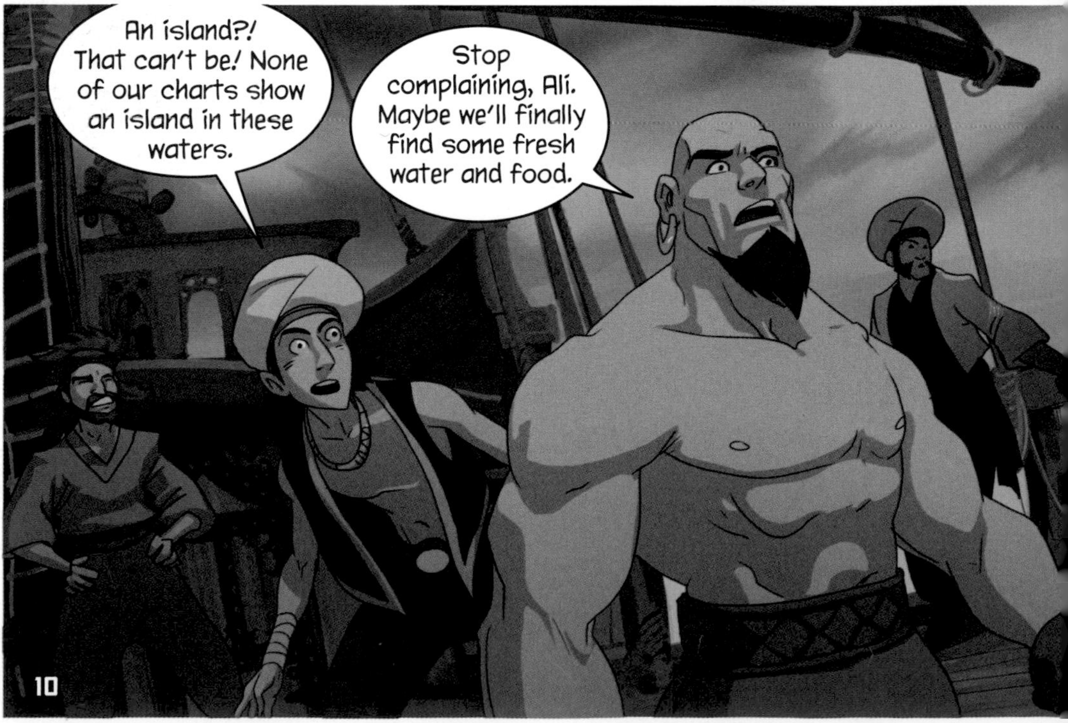
An island?! That can't be! None of our charts show an island in these waters.
Stop complaining, Ali. Maybe we'll finally find some fresh water and food.

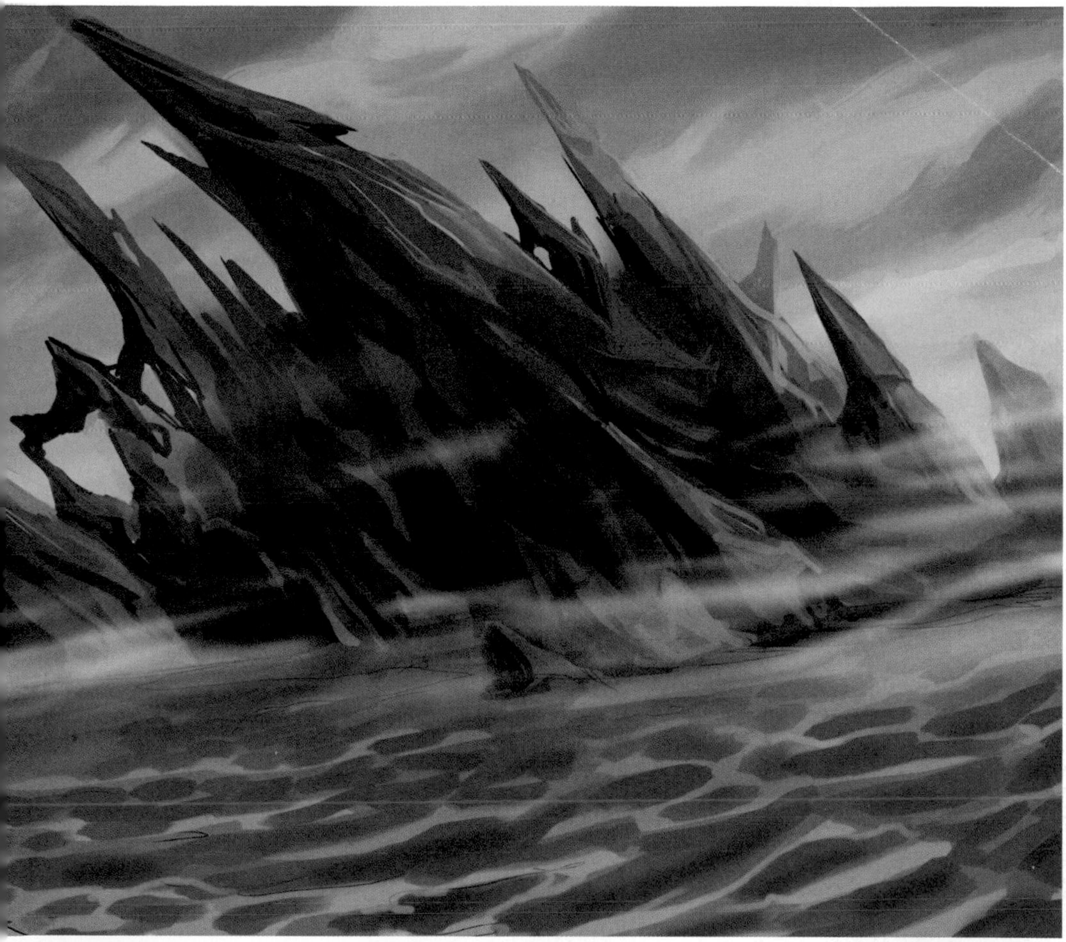

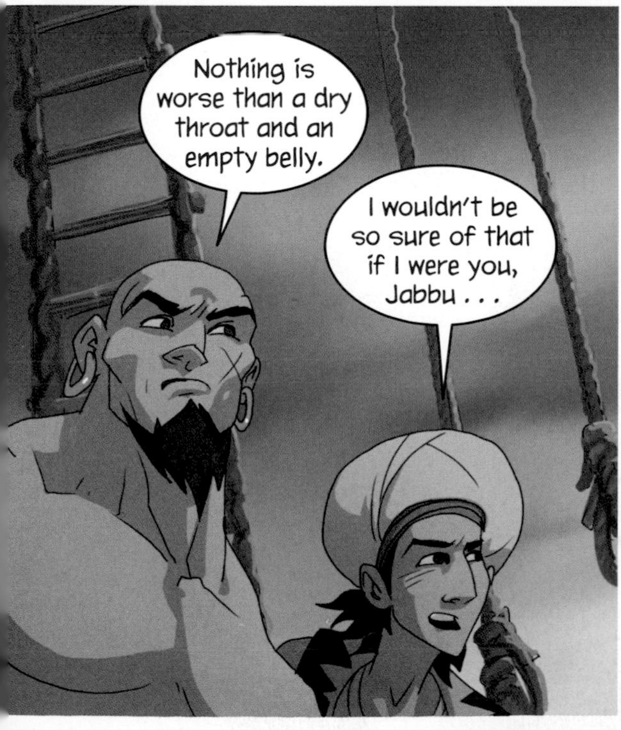
Nothing is worse than a dry throat and an empty belly.
I wouldn't be so sure of that if I were you, Jabbu . . .

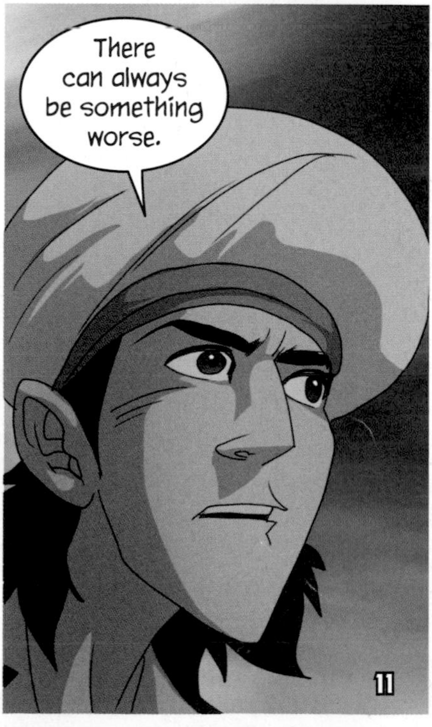
There can always be something worse.

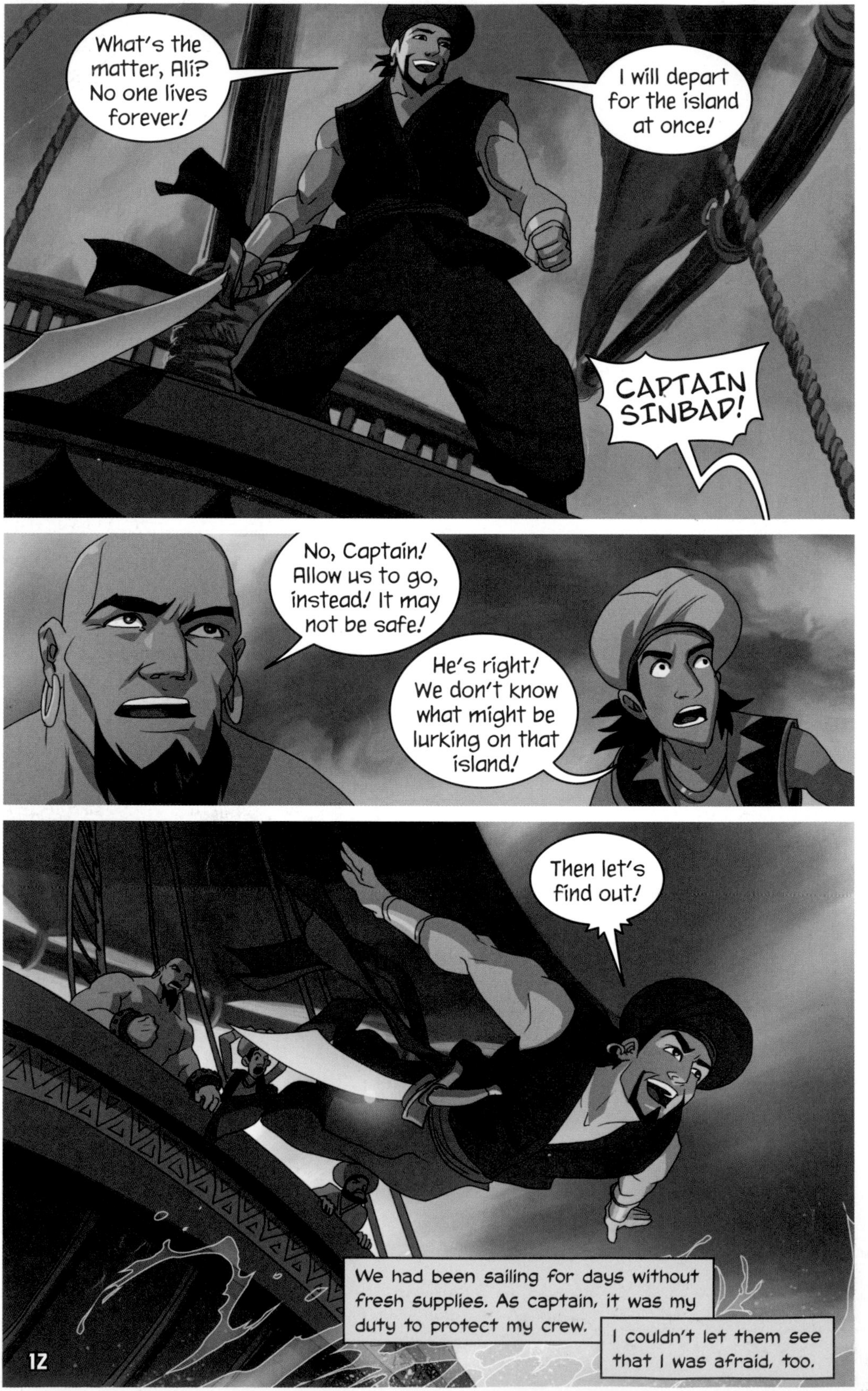
What's the matter, Ali? No one lives forever!
I will depart for the island at once!
CAPTAIN SINBAD!
No, Captain! Allow us to go, instead! It may not be safe!
He's right! We don't know what might be lurking on that island!
Then let's find out!
We had been sailing for days without fresh supplies. As captain, it was my duty to protect my crew.
I couldn't let them see that I was afraid, too.

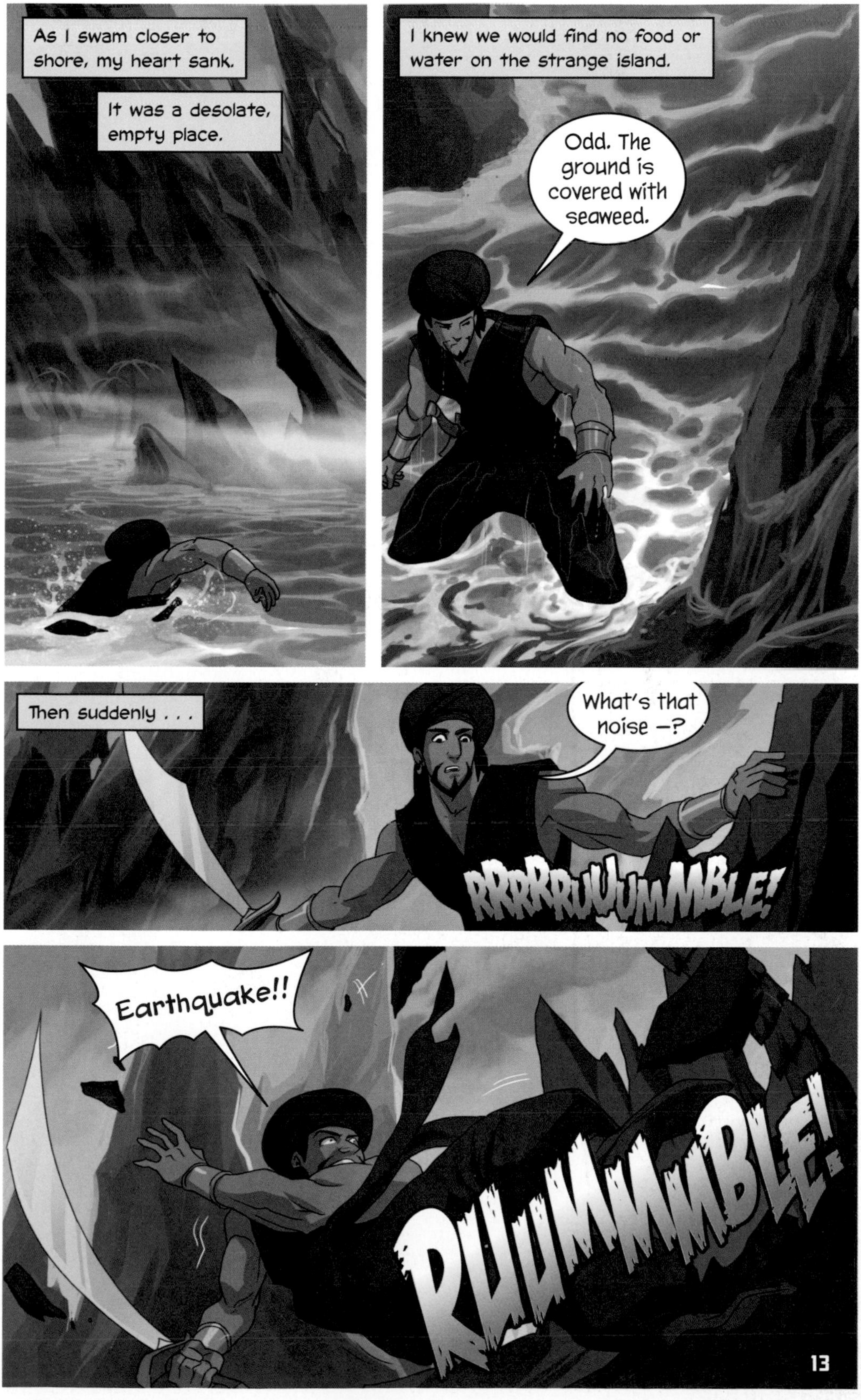
As I swam closer to shore, my heart sank.
It was a desolate, empty place.
I knew we would find no food or water on the strange island.
Odd. The ground is covered with seaweed.
Then suddenly . . .
What's that noise —?
RRRRRRUUUUMMBLE!
Earthquake!!
RUUMMMBLE!

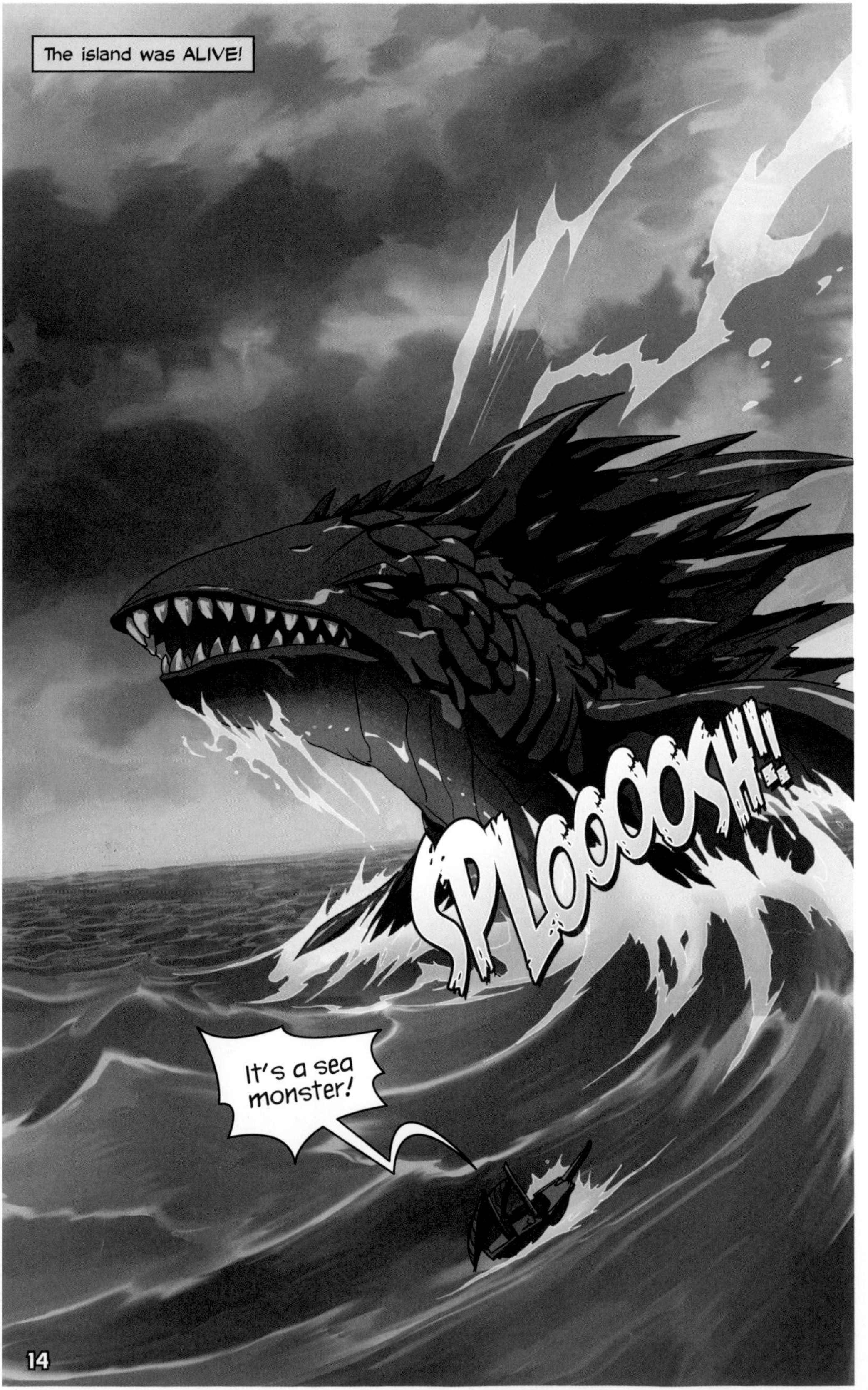
The island was ALIVE!
SPLOOOOSH!!
It's a sea monster!

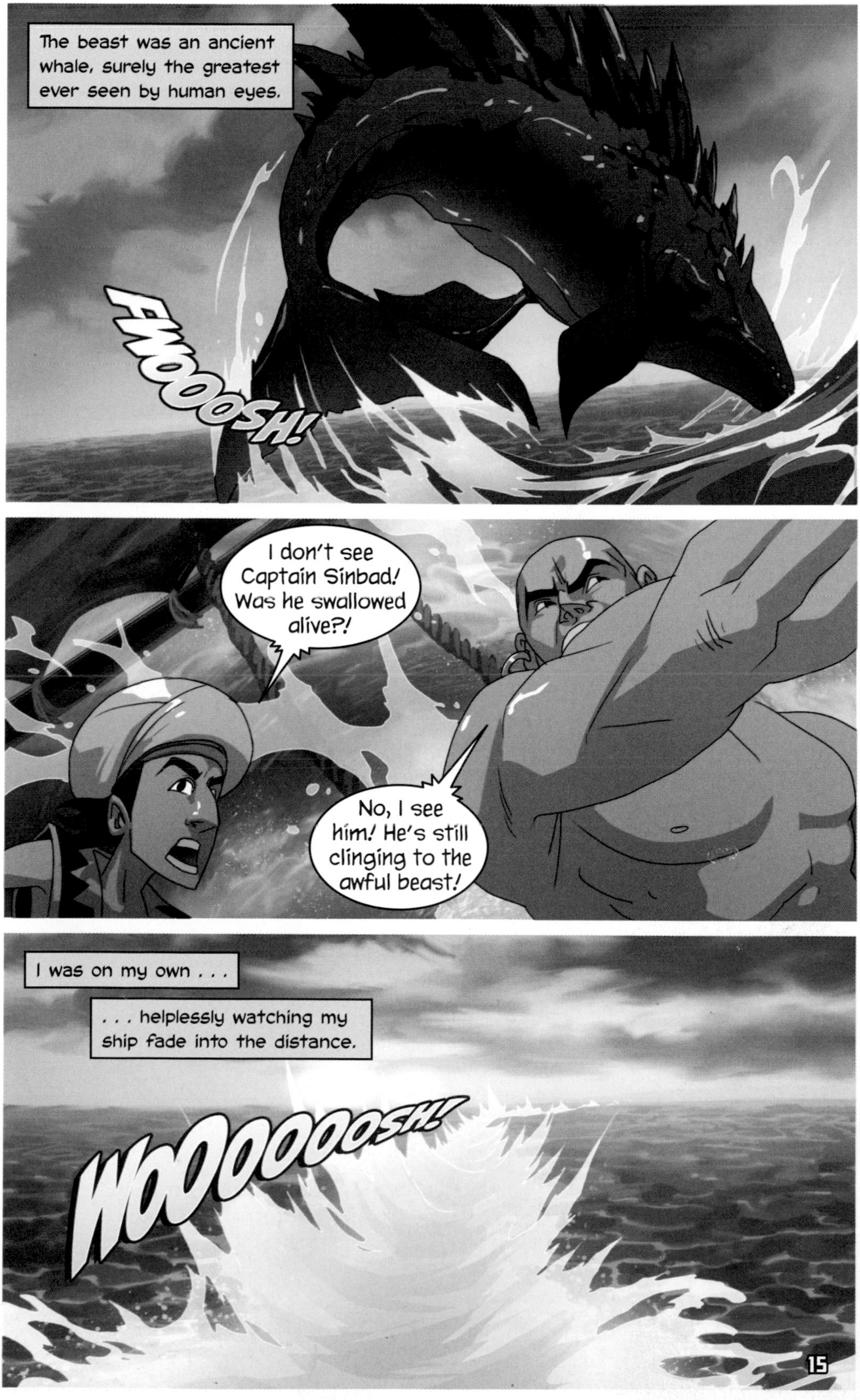
The beast was an ancient whale, surely the greatest ever seen by human eyes.
FWOOOSH!
I don't see Captain Sinbad! Was he swallowed alive?!
No, I see him! He's still clinging to the awful beast!
I was on my own . . .
. . . helplessly watching my ship fade into the distance.
WOOOOOOSH!

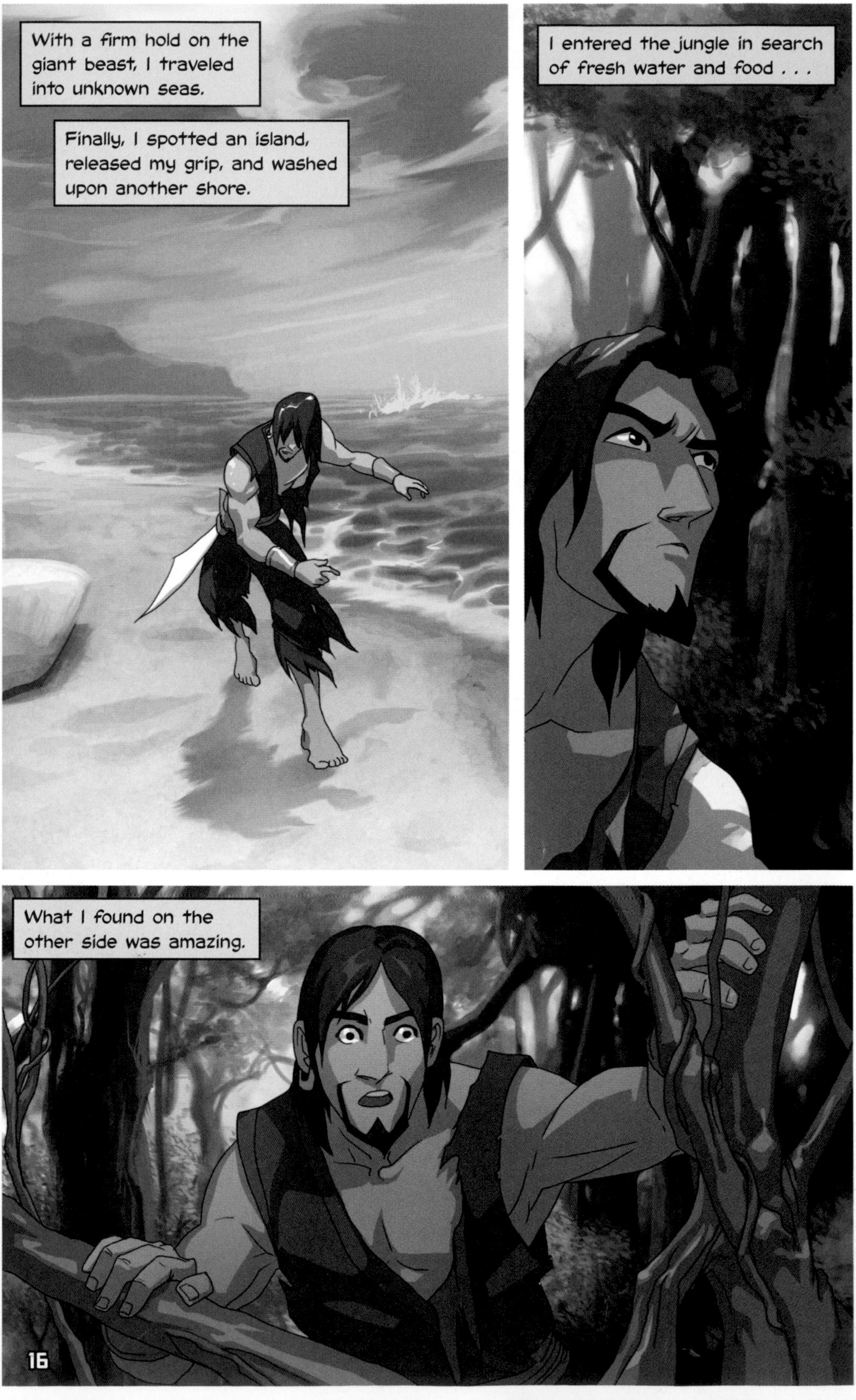
With a firm hold on the giant beast, I traveled into unknown seas.
Finally, I spotted an island, released my grip, and washed upon another shore.
I entered the jungle in search of fresh water and food . . .
What I found on the other side was amazing.

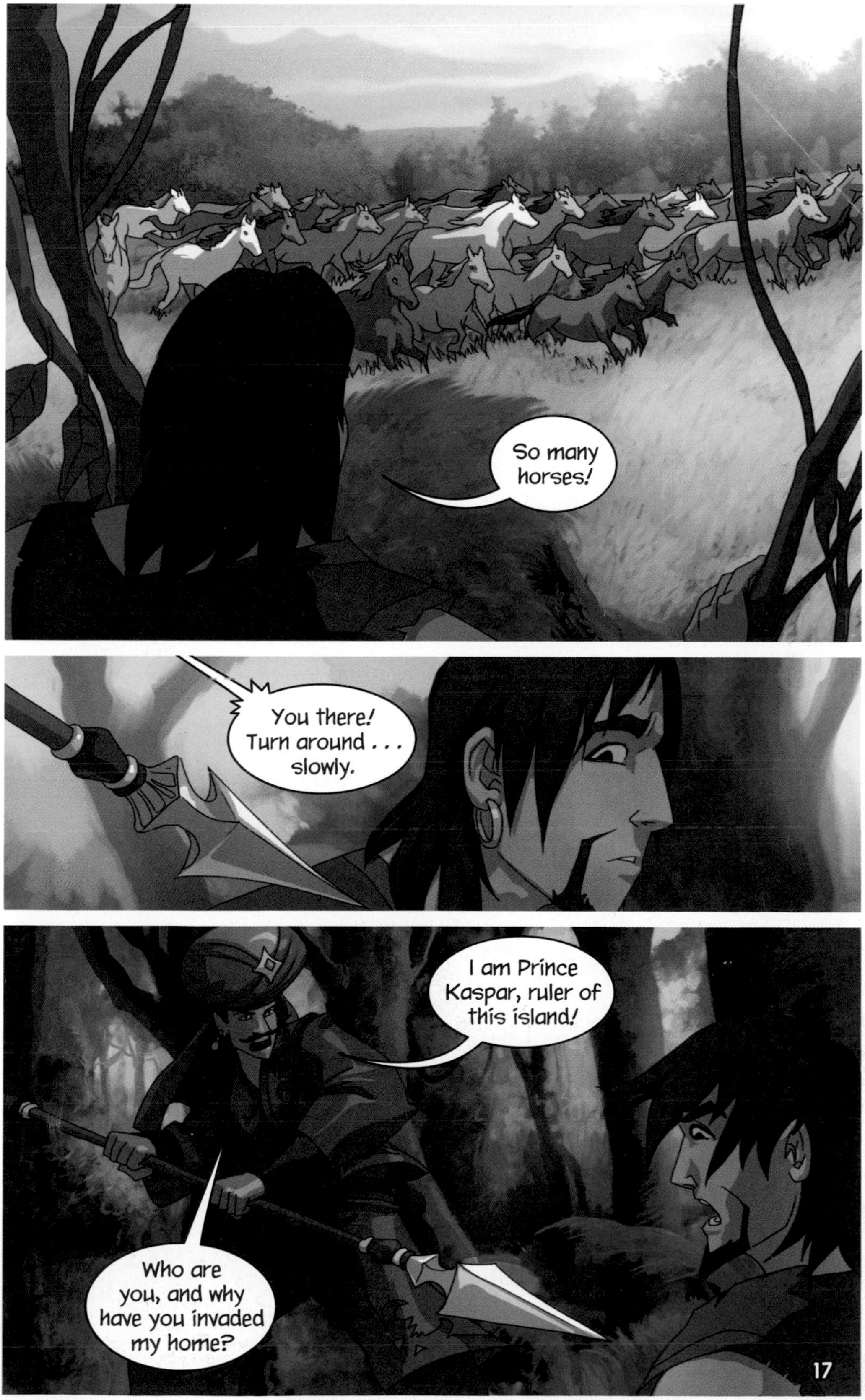
So many horses!
You there! Turn around . . . slowly.
I am Prince Kaspar, ruler of this island!
Who are you, and why have you invaded my home?

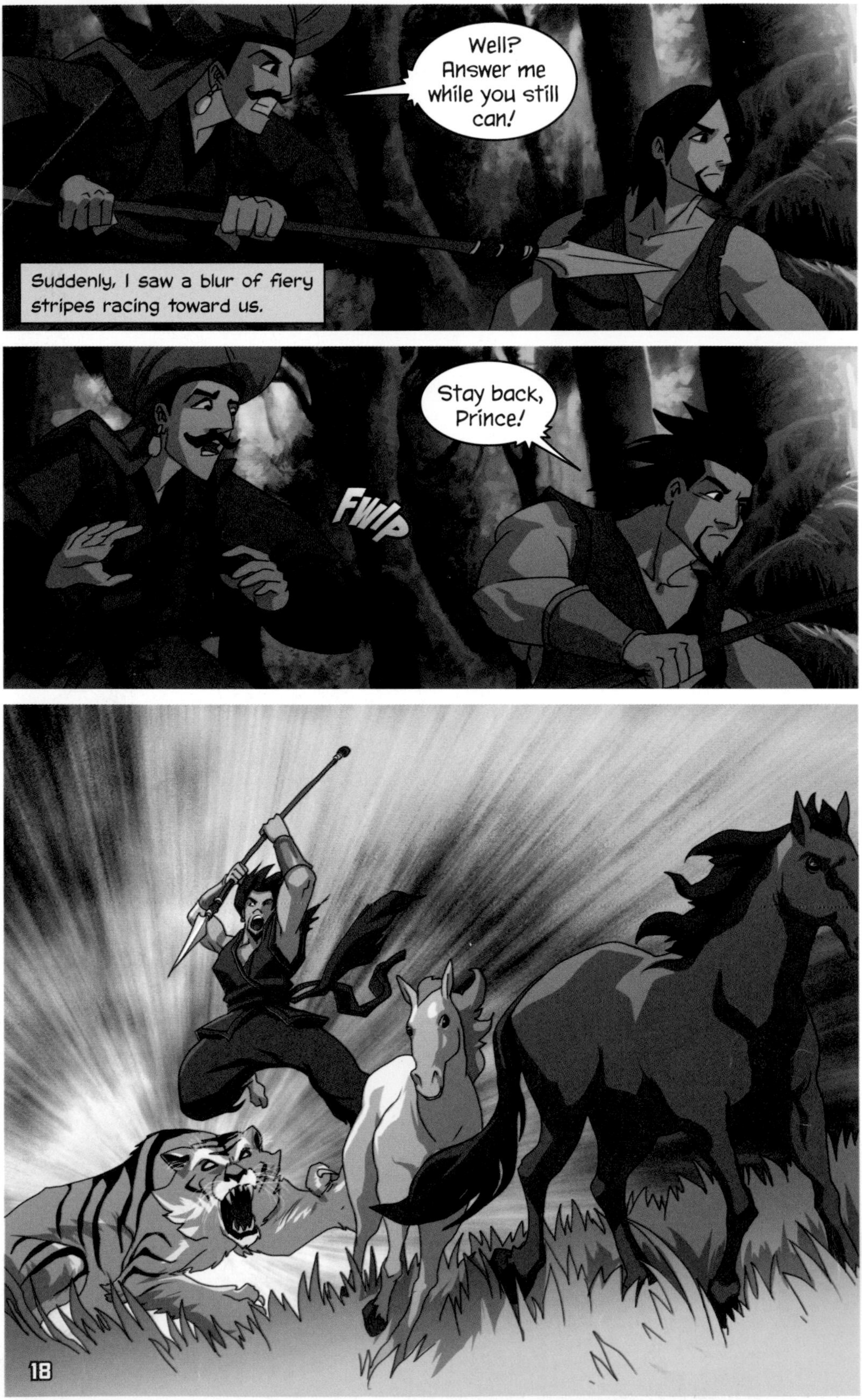
Well? Answer me while you still can!
Suddenly, I saw a blur of fiery stripes racing toward us.
Stay back, Prince!
FWIP

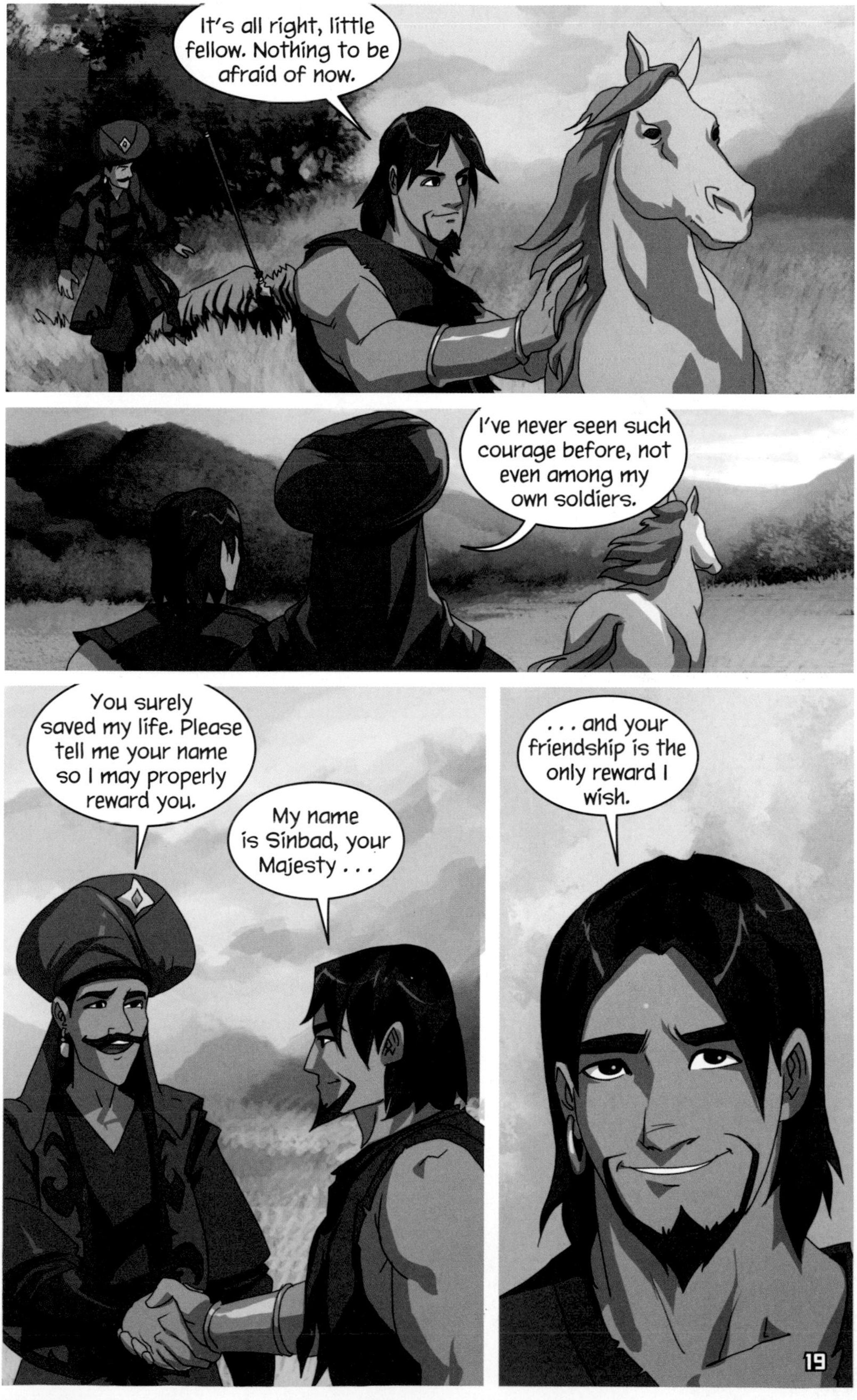
It's all right, little fellow. Nothing to be afraid of now.
I've never seen such courage before, not even among my own soldiers.
You surely saved my life. Please tell me your name so I may properly reward you.
My name is Sinbad, your Majesty . . .
. . . and your friendship is the only reward I wish.

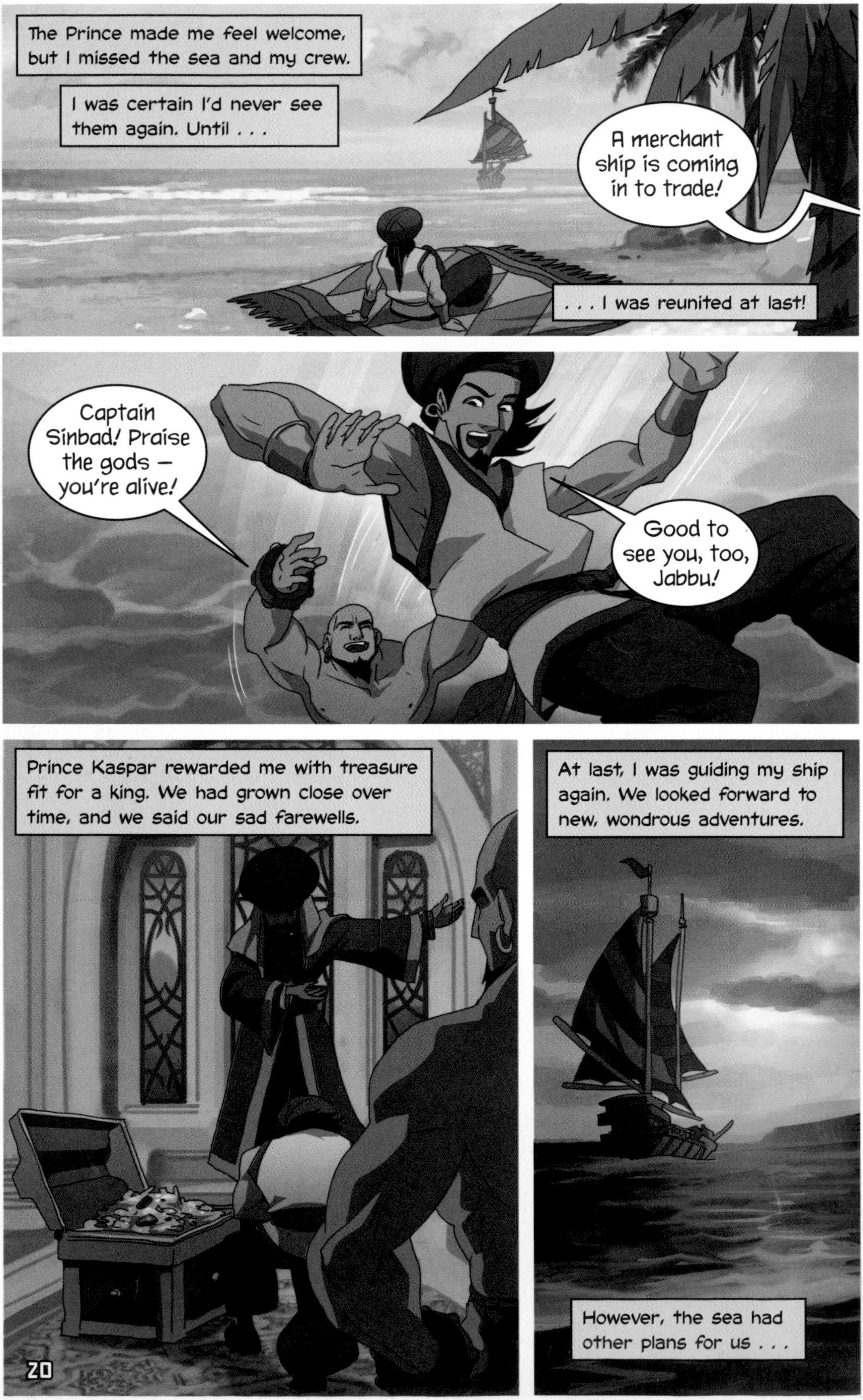
The Prince made me feel welcome, but I missed the sea and my crew.
I was certain I'd never see them again. Until . . .
A merchant ship is coming in to trade!
. . . I was reunited at last!
Captain Sinbad! Praise the gods — you're alive!
Good to see you, too, Jabbu!
Prince Kaspar rewarded me with treasure fit for a king. We had grown close over time, and we said our sad farewells.
At last, I was guiding my ship again. We looked forward to new, wondrous adventures.
However, the sea had other plans for us . . .

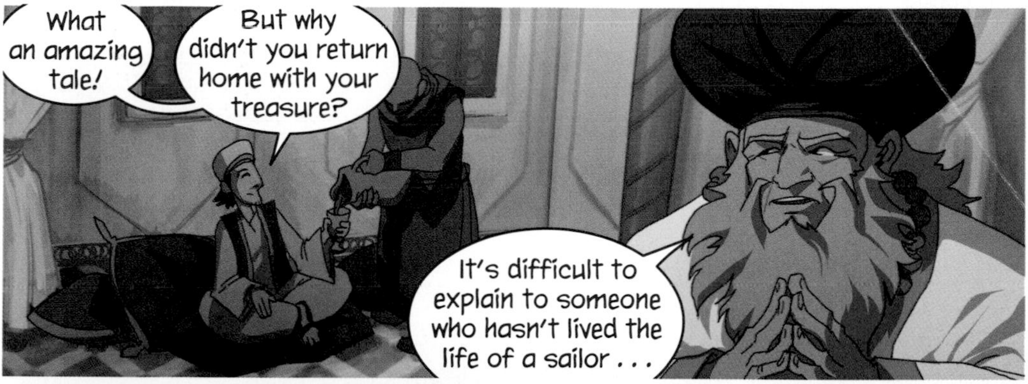
What an amazing tale!
But why didn't you return home with your treasure?
It's difficult to explain to someone who hasn't lived the life of a sailor . . .

CHAPTER TWO:
THE SECOND VOYAGE

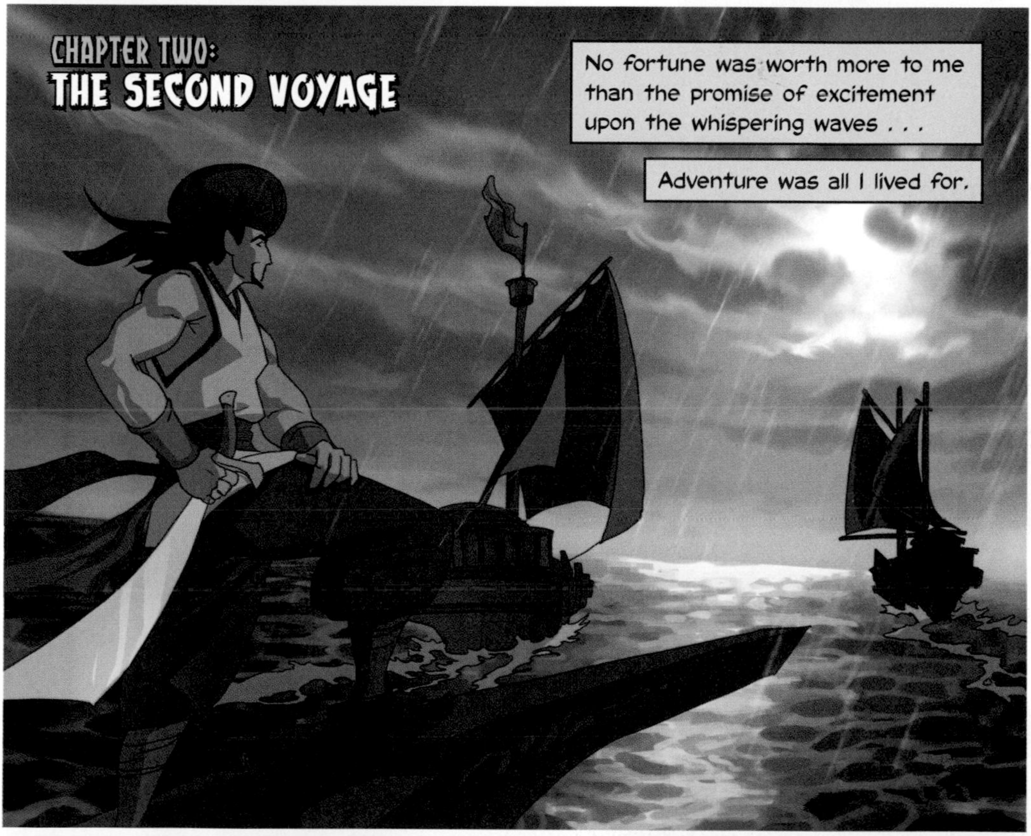
No fortune was worth more to me than the promise of excitement upon the whispering waves . . .
Adventure was all I lived for.

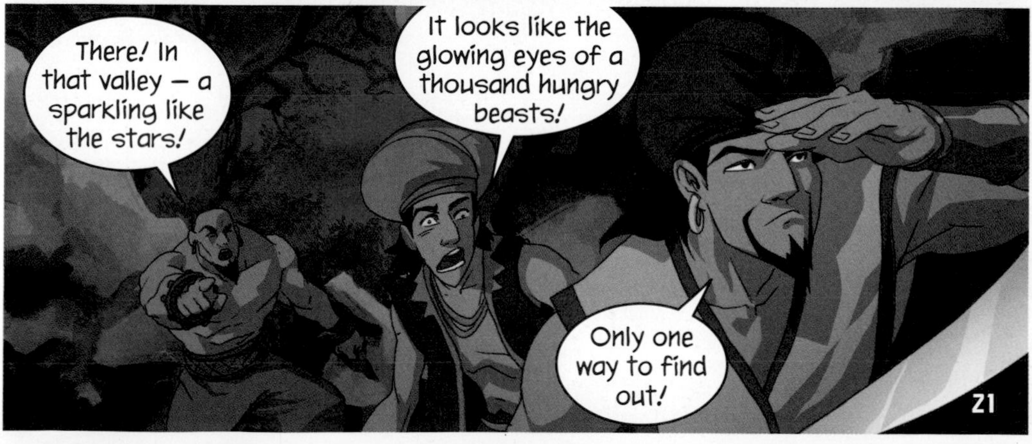
There! In that valley — a sparkling like the stars!
It looks like the glowing eyes of a thousand hungry beasts!
Only one way to find out!

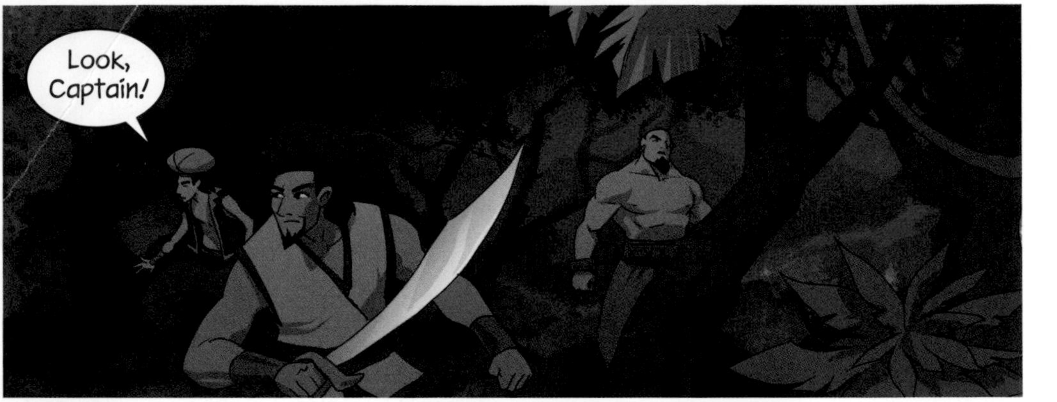
Look, Captain!

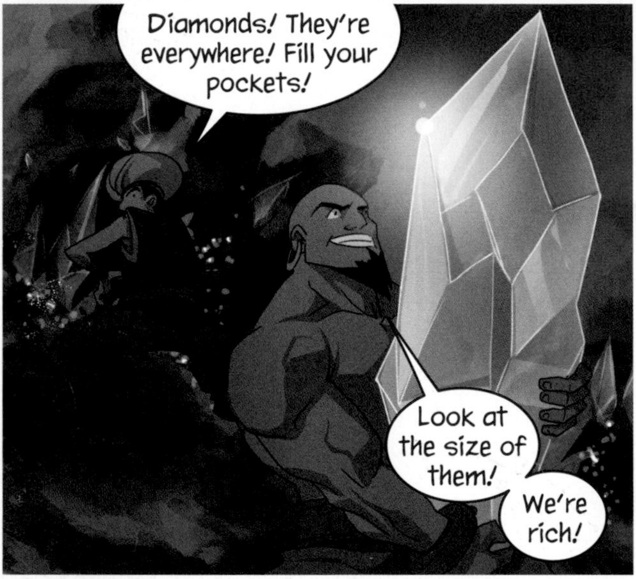
Diamonds! They're everywhere! Fill your pockets!
Look at the size of them!
We're rich!

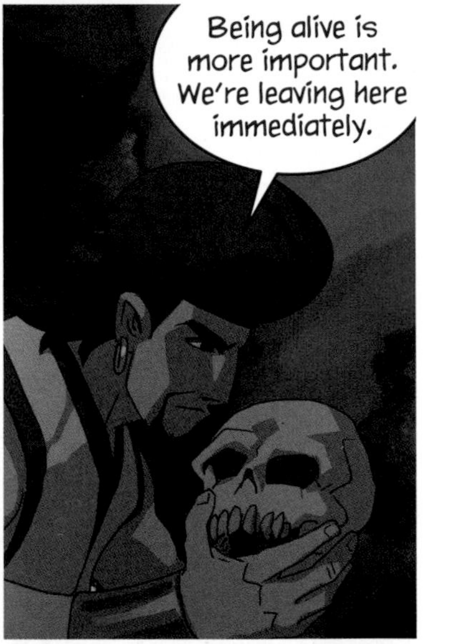
Being alive is more important. We're leaving here immediately.

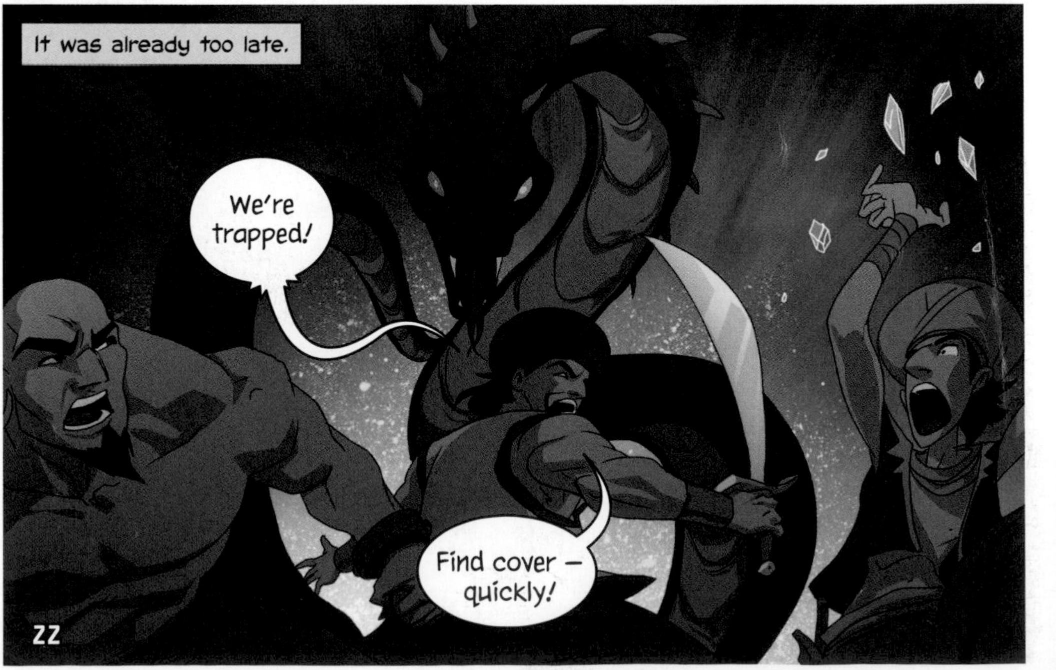
It was already too late.
We're trapped!
Find cover — quickly!

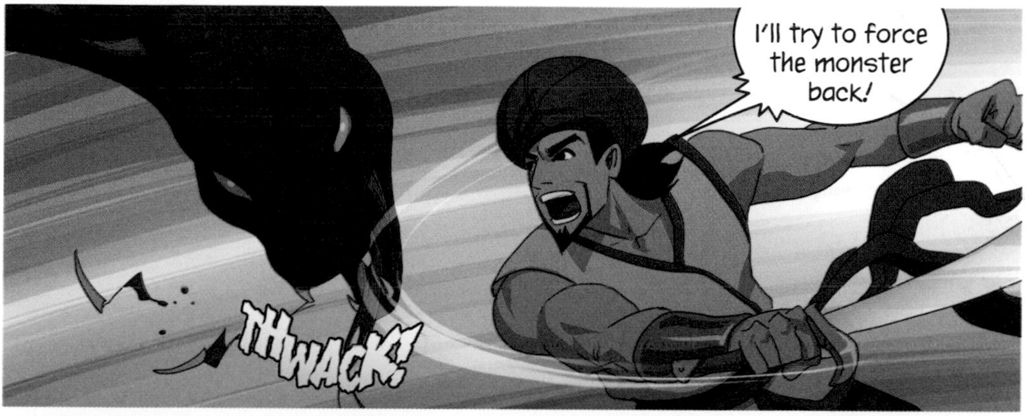
I'll try to force the monster back!
THWACK!

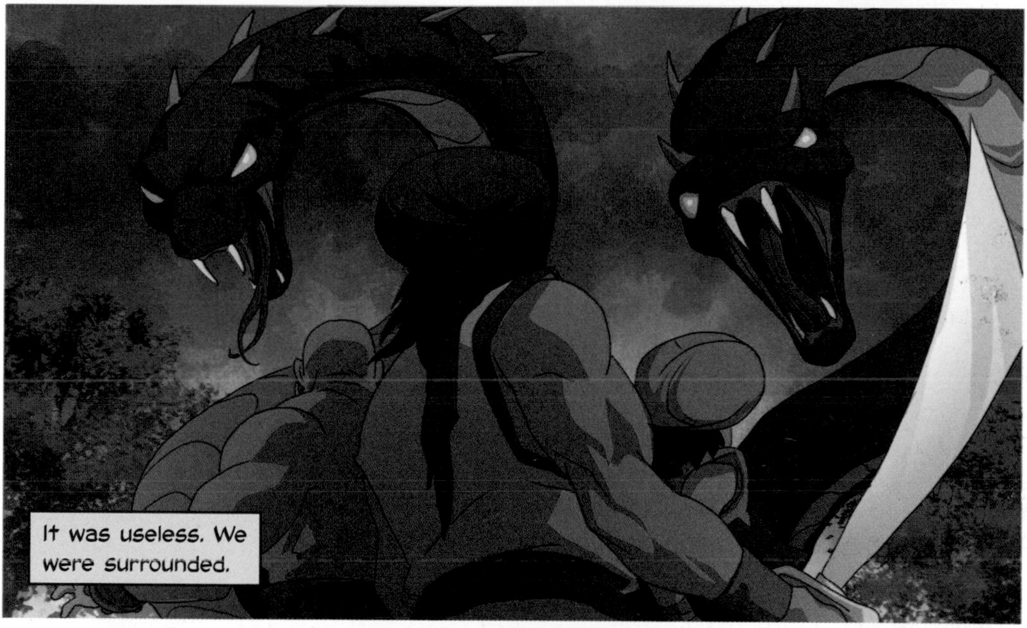
It was useless. We were surrounded.

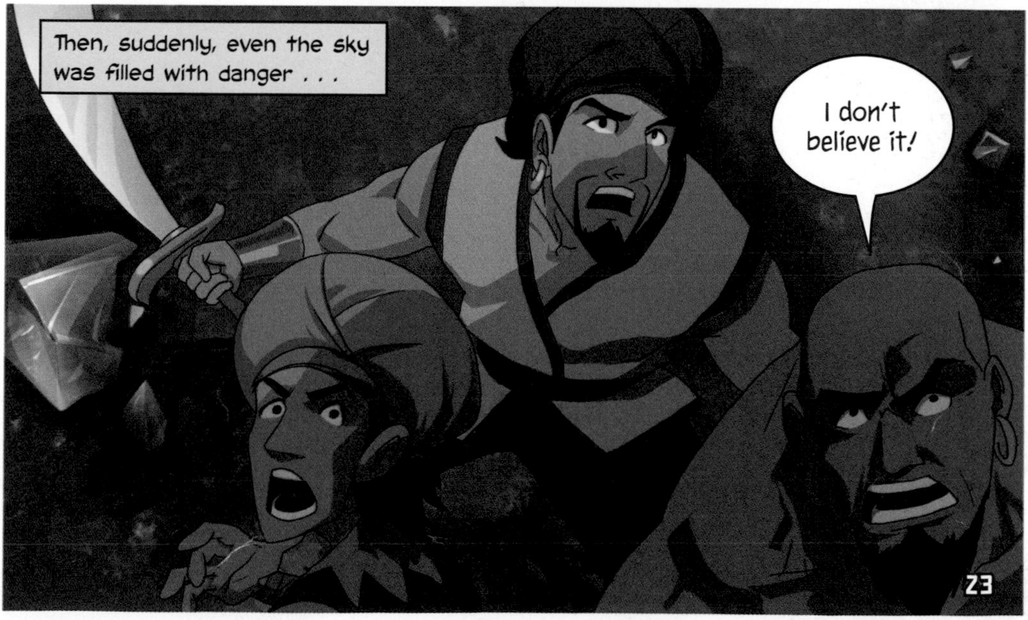
Then, suddenly, even the sky was filled with danger . . .
I don't believe it!

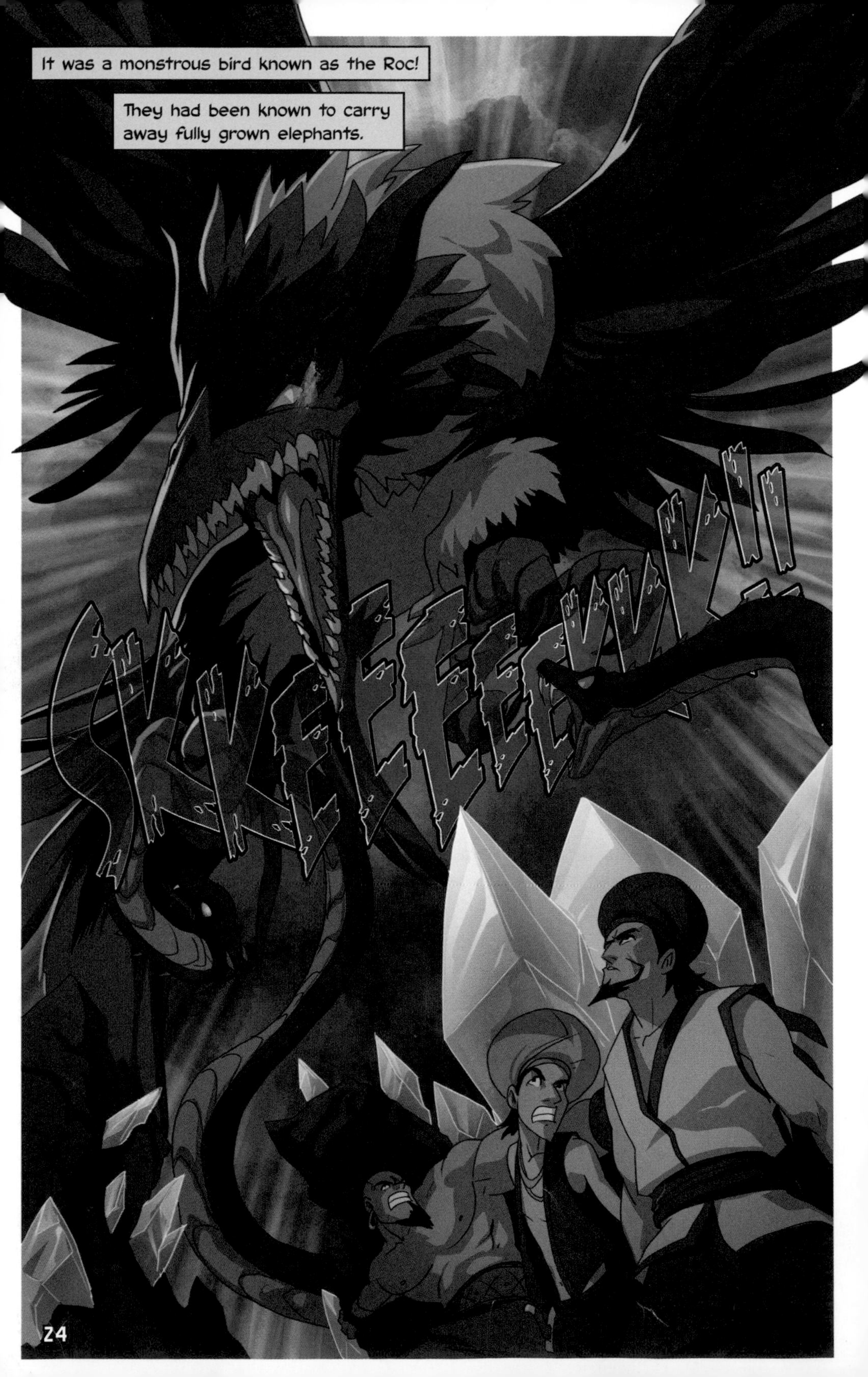
It was a monstrous bird known as the Roc!
They had been known to carry away fully grown elephants.

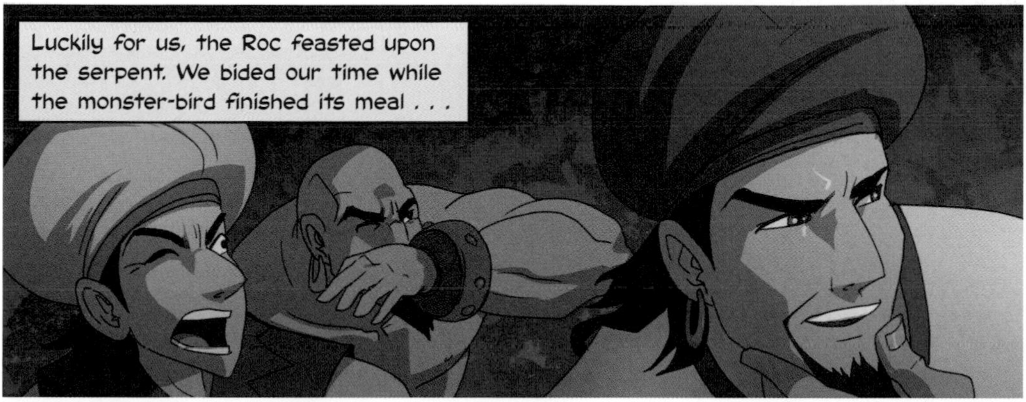
Luckily for us, the Roc feasted upon the serpent. We bided our time while the monster-bird finished its meal . . .
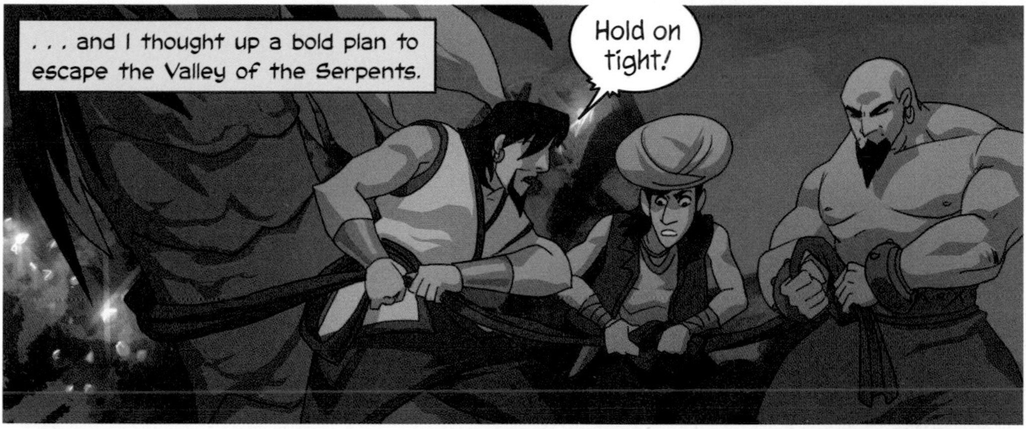
. . . and I thought up a bold plan to escape the Valley of the Serpents.
Hold on tight!
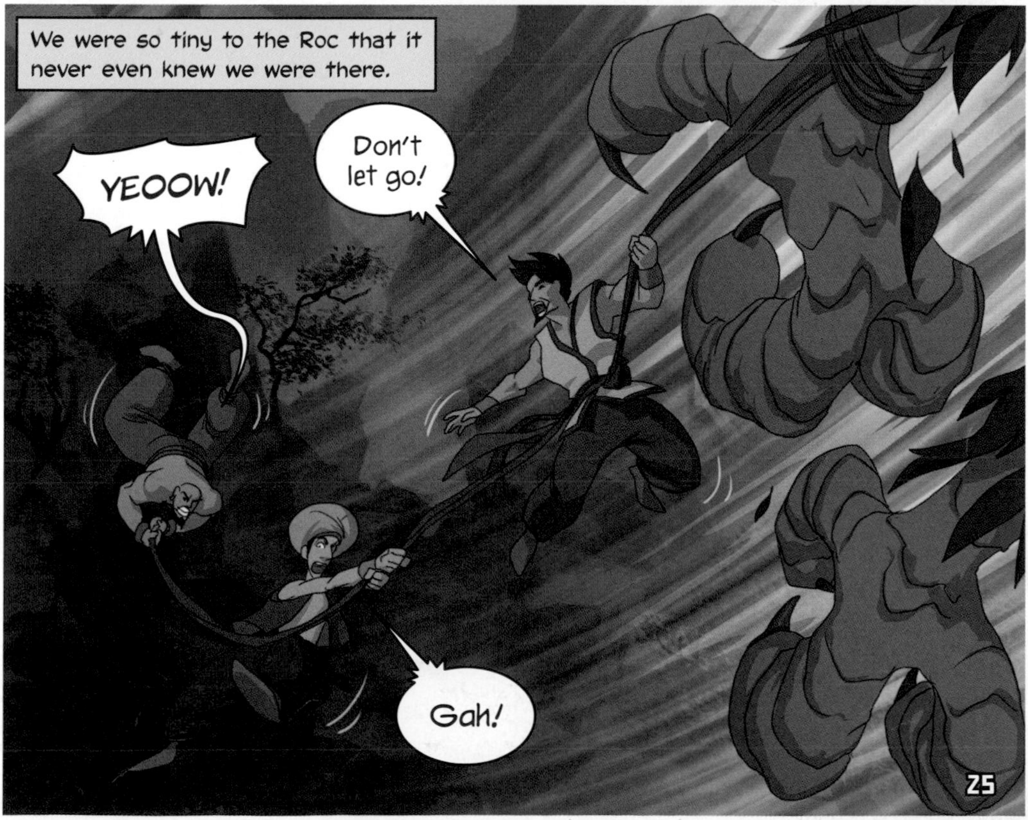
We were so tiny to the Roc that it never even knew we were there.
YEOOW!
Don't let go!
Gah!

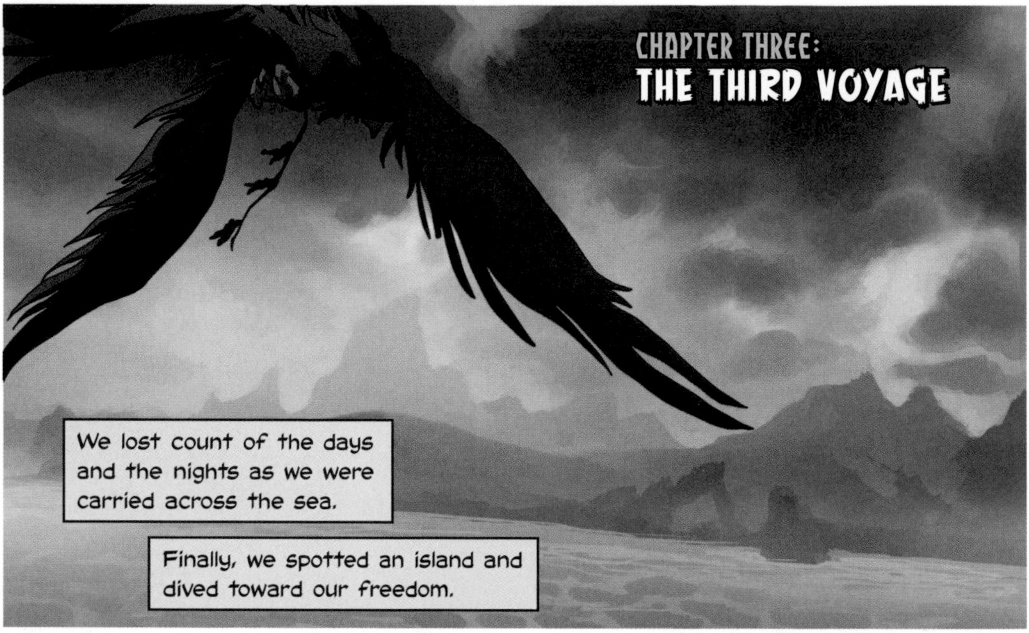
CHAPTER THREE:
THE THIRD VOYAGE
We lost count of the days and the nights as we were carried across the sea.
Finally, we spotted an island and dived toward our freedom.

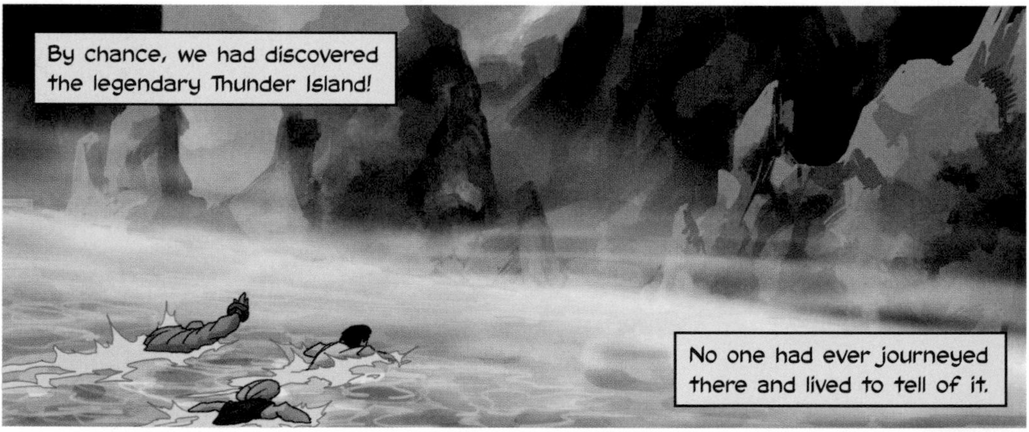
By chance, we had discovered the legendary Thunder Island!
No one had ever journeyed there and lived to tell of it.

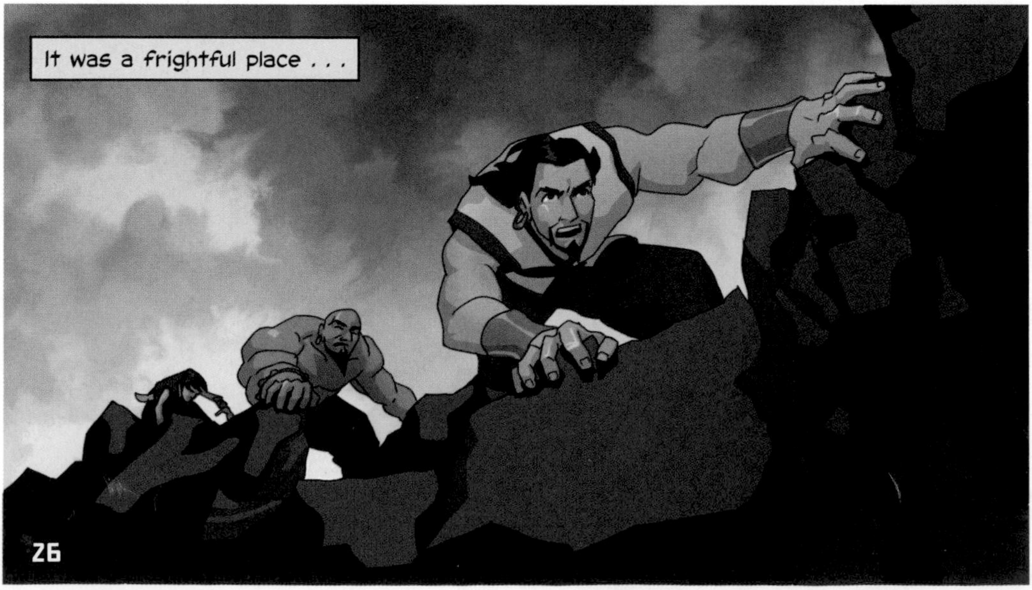
It was a frightful place . . .

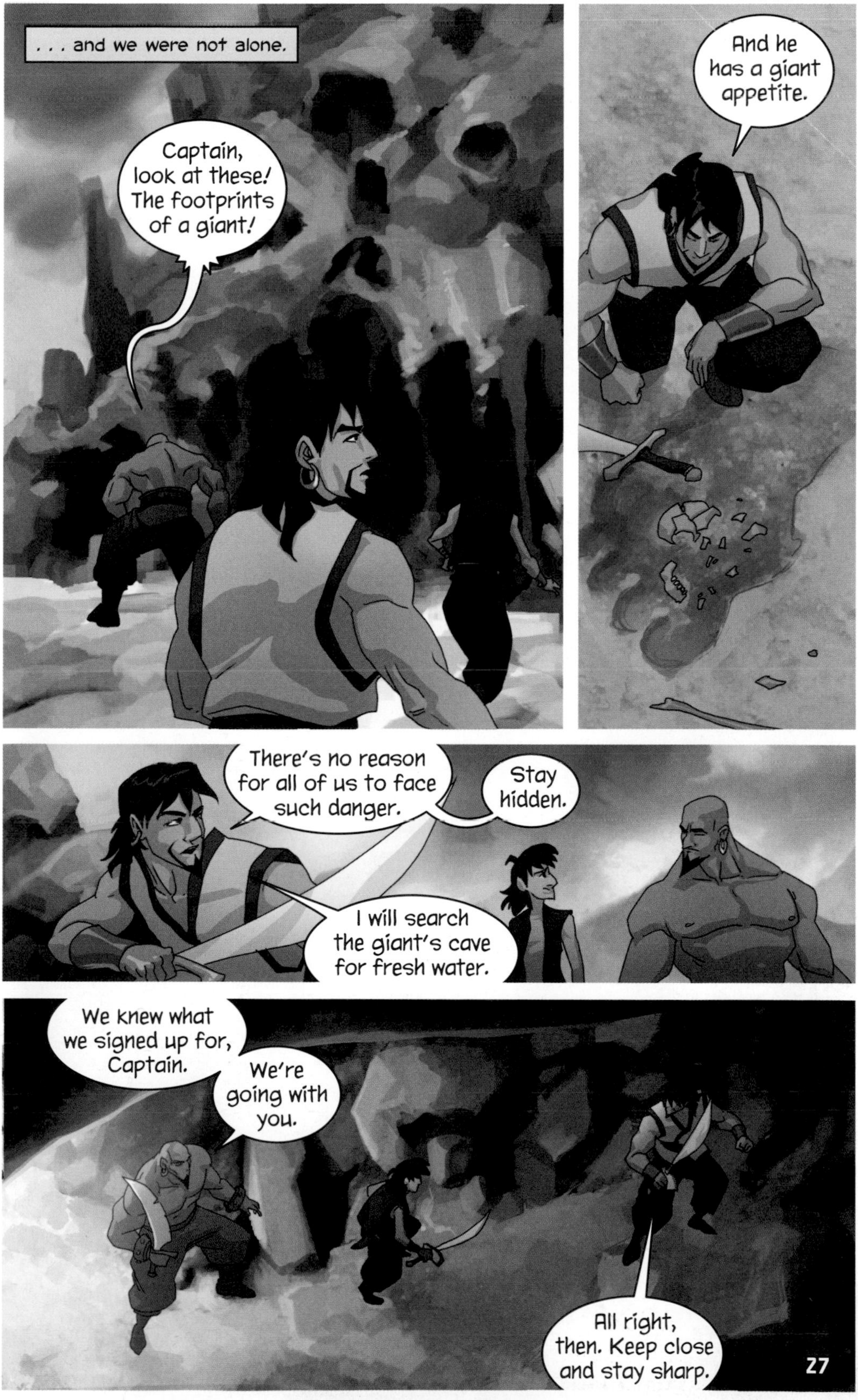
. . . and we were not alone.
Captain, look at these! The footprints of a giant!
And he has a giant appetite.
There's no reason for all of us to face such danger.
Stay hidden.
I will search the giant's cave for fresh water.
We knew what we signed up for, Captain.
We're going with you.
All right, then. Keep close and stay sharp.

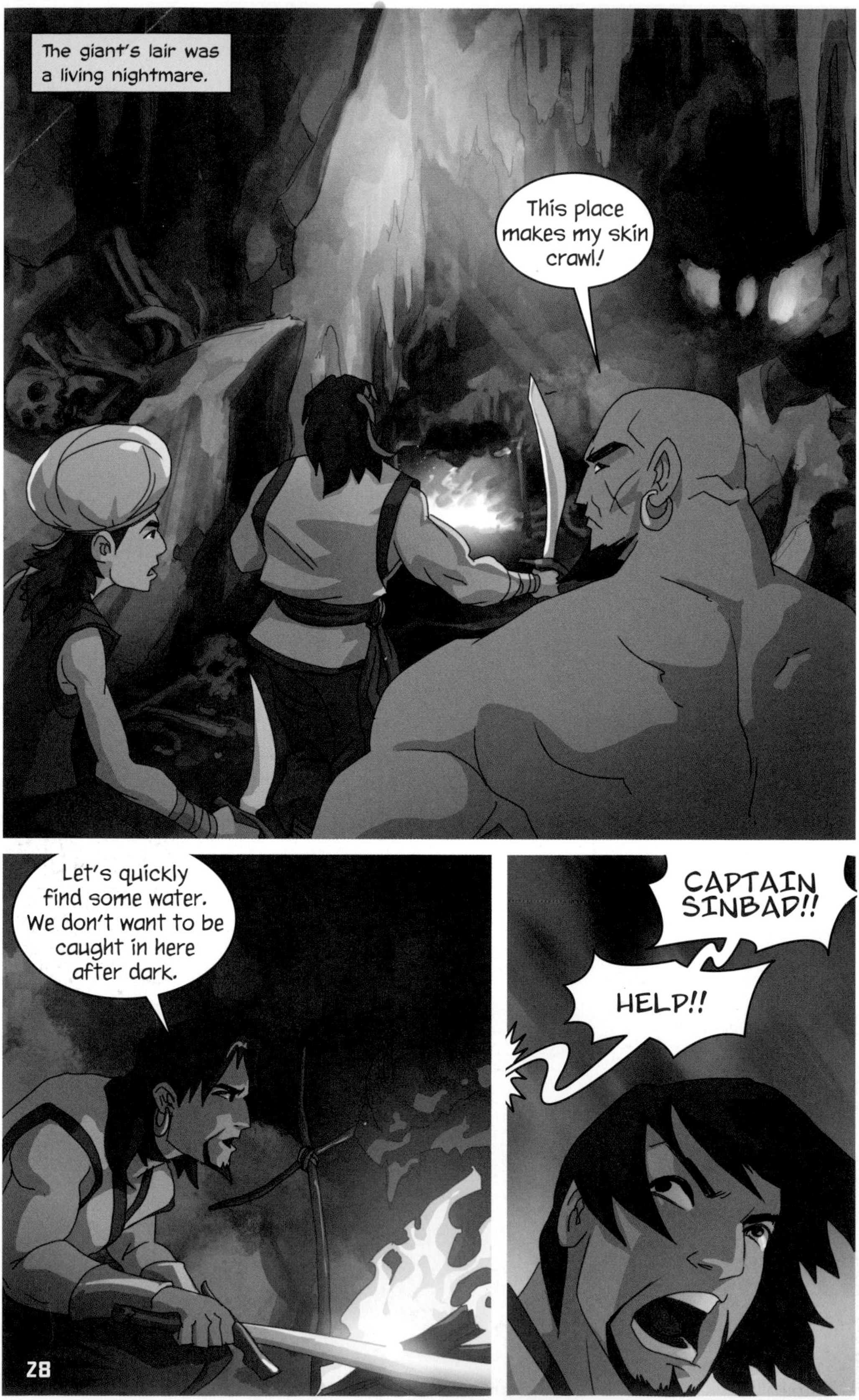
The giant's lair was a living nightmare.
This place makes my skin crawl!
Let's quickly find some water. We don't want to be caught in here after dark.
CAPTAIN SINBAD!!
HELP!!

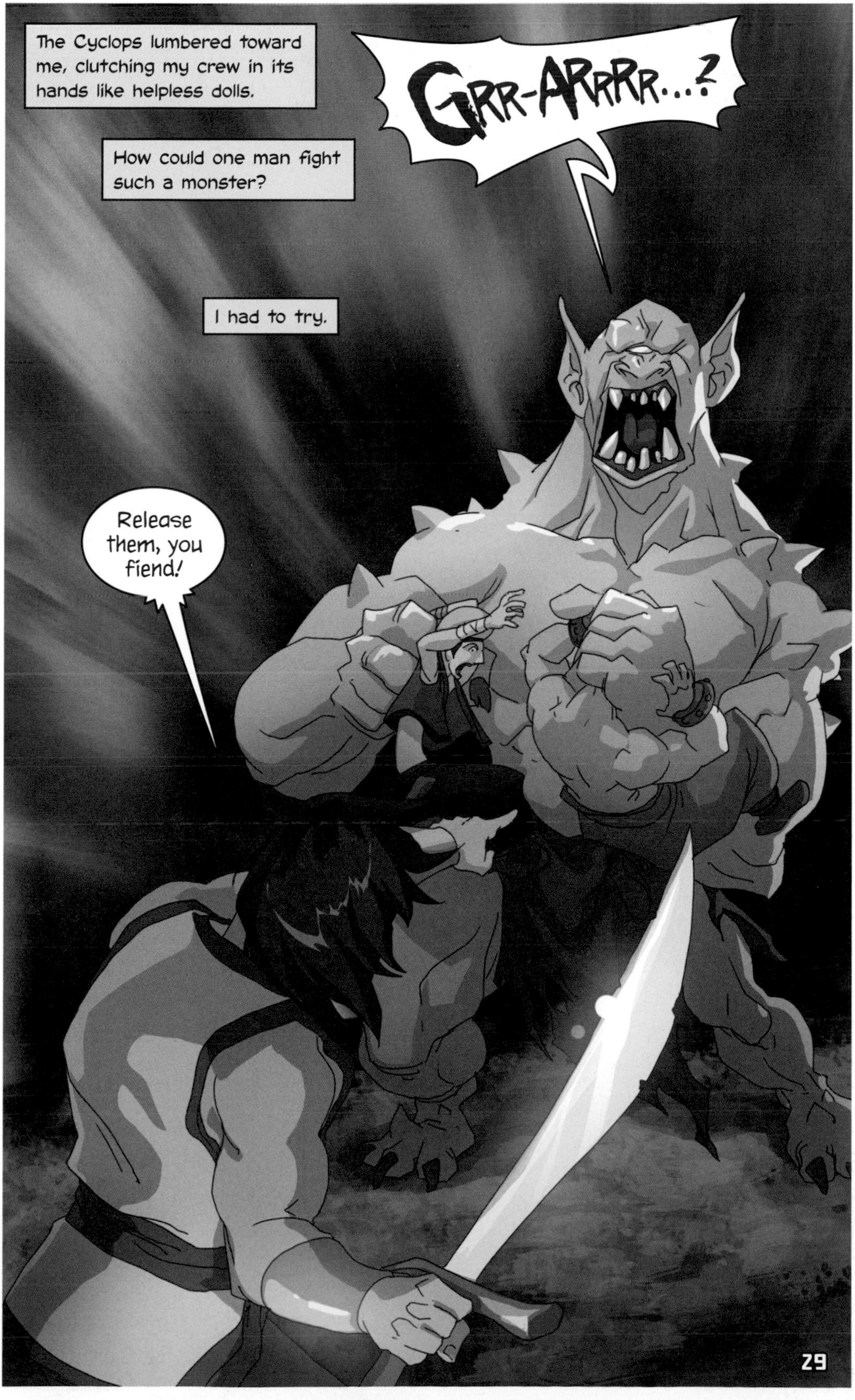
The Cyclops lumbered toward me, clutching my crew in its hands like helpless dolls.
GRR-ARRRR...?
How could one man fight such a monster?
I had to try.
Release them, you fiend!

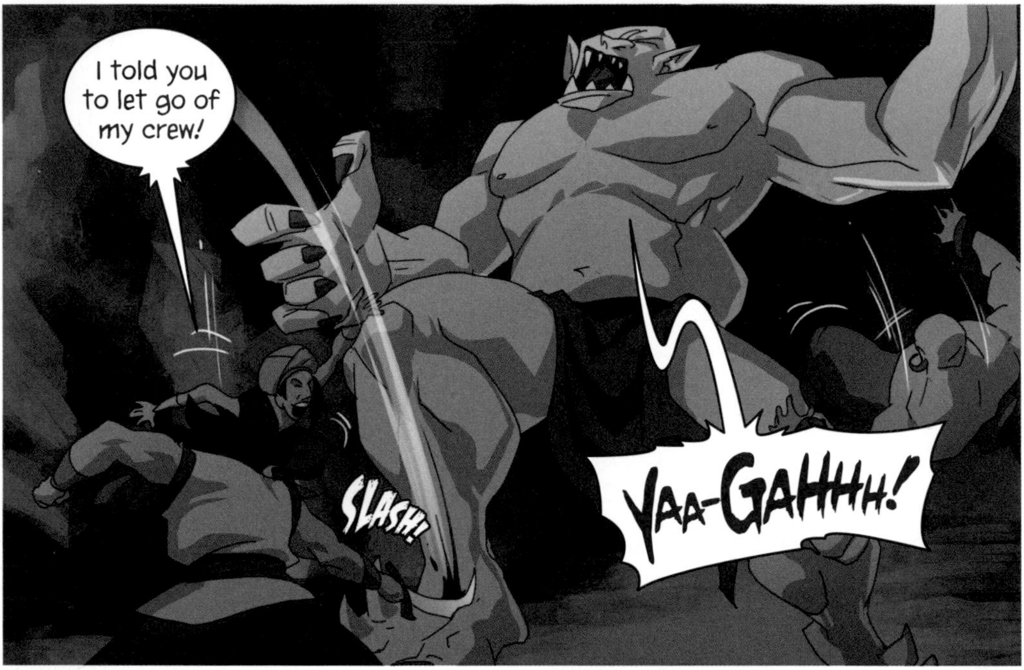
I told you to let go of my crew!
SLASH!
YAA-GAHHH!

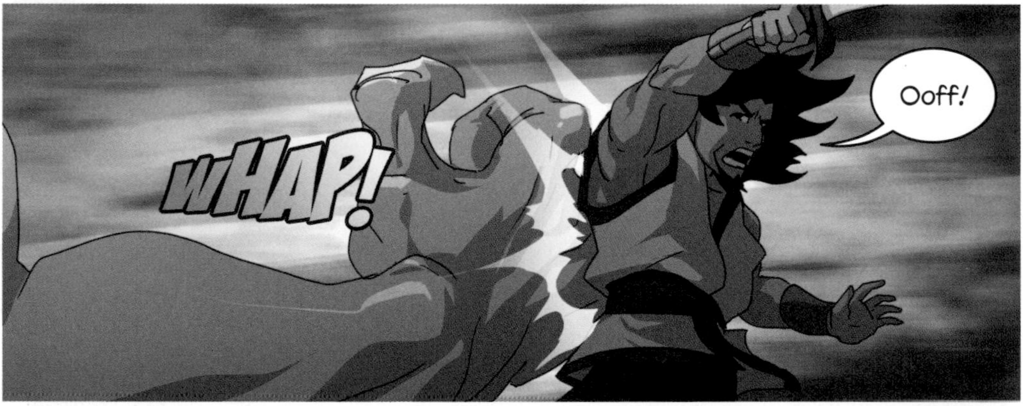
WHAP!
Ooff!

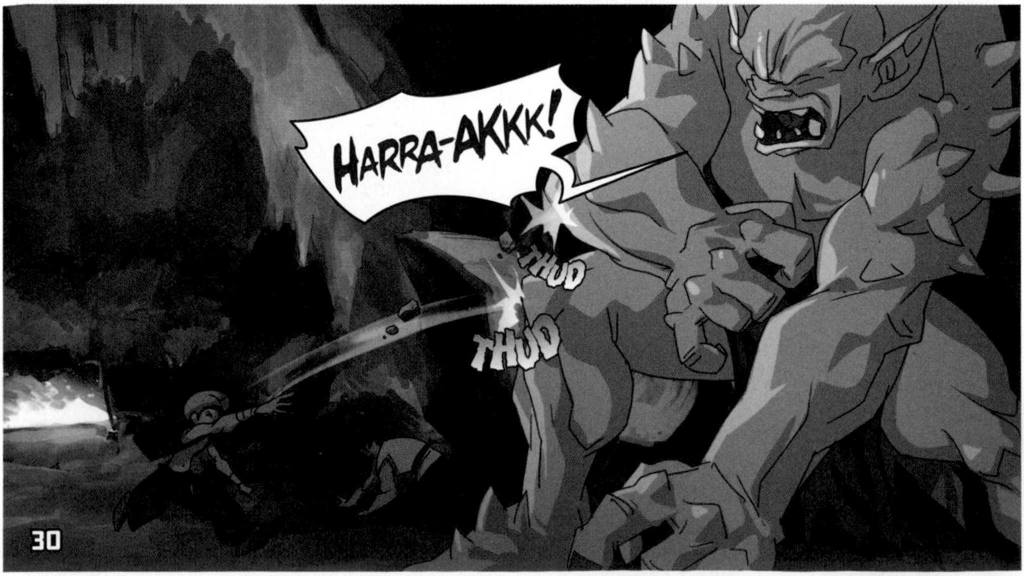
HARRA-AKKK!
THUD
THUD

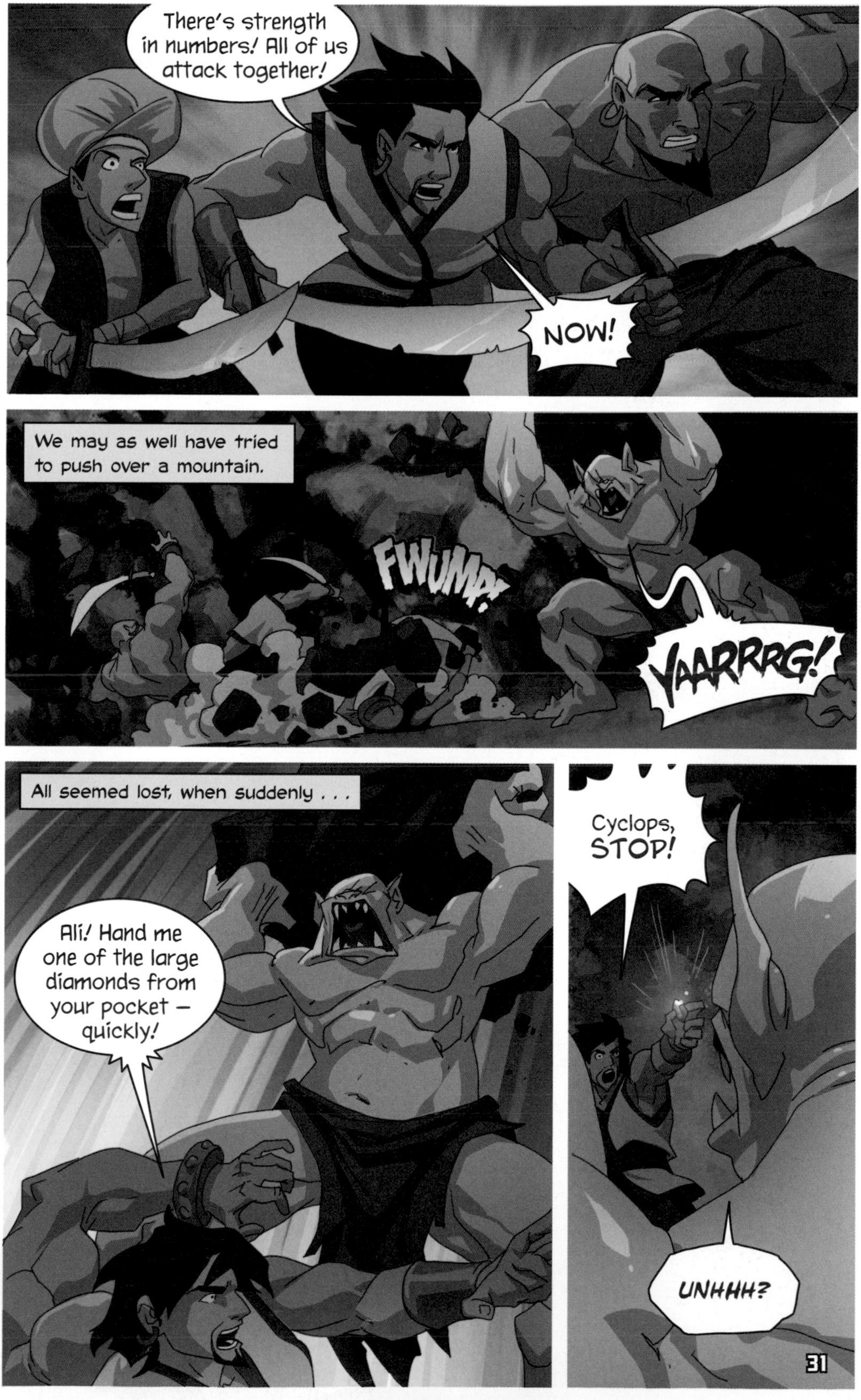
There's strength in numbers! All of us attack together!
NOW!
We may as well have tried to push over a mountain.
FWUMP!
YAARRRG!
All seemed lost, when suddenly . . .
Ali! Hand me one of the large diamonds from your pocket — quickly!
Cyclops, STOP!
UNHHH?

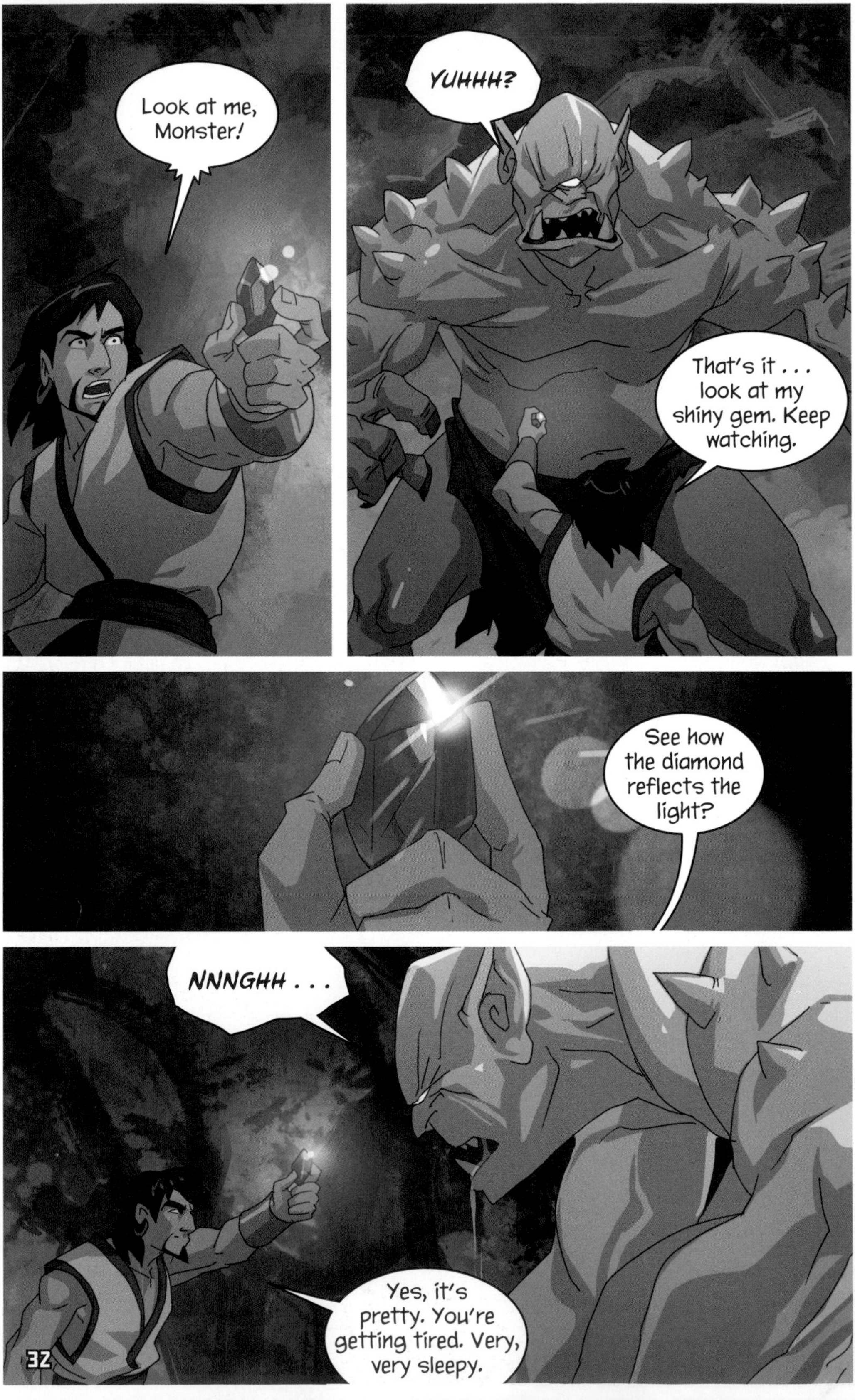
Look at me, Monster!
YUHHH?
That's it . . . look at my shiny gem. Keep watching.
See how the diamond reflects the light?
NNNGHH . . .
Yes, it's pretty. You're getting tired. Very, very sleepy.

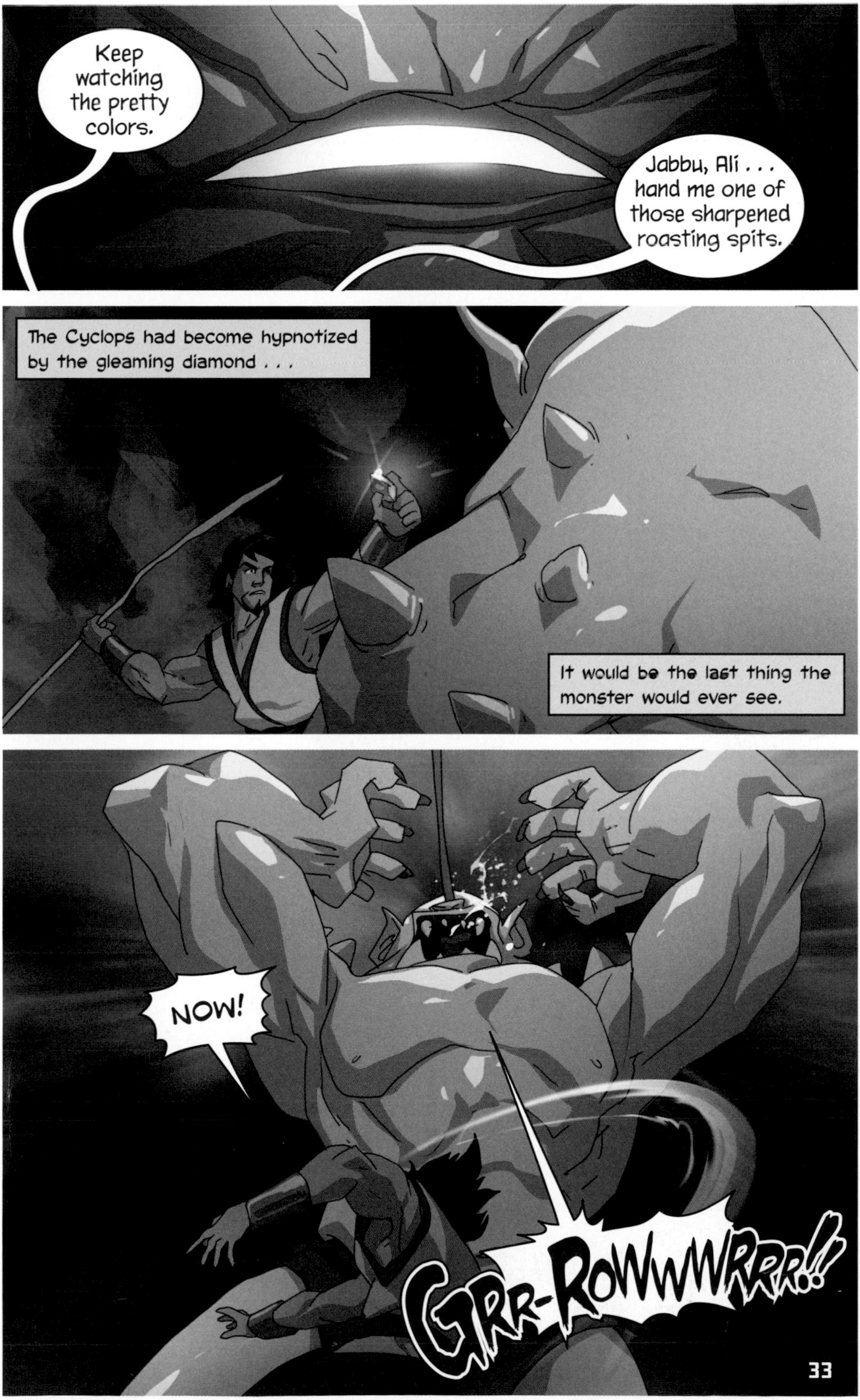
Keep watching the pretty colors.
Jabbu, Ali . . . hand me one of those sharpened roasting spits.
The Cyclops had become hypnotized by the gleaming diamond . . .
It would be the last thing the monster would ever see.
NOW!
GRR-ROWWWRRR!!

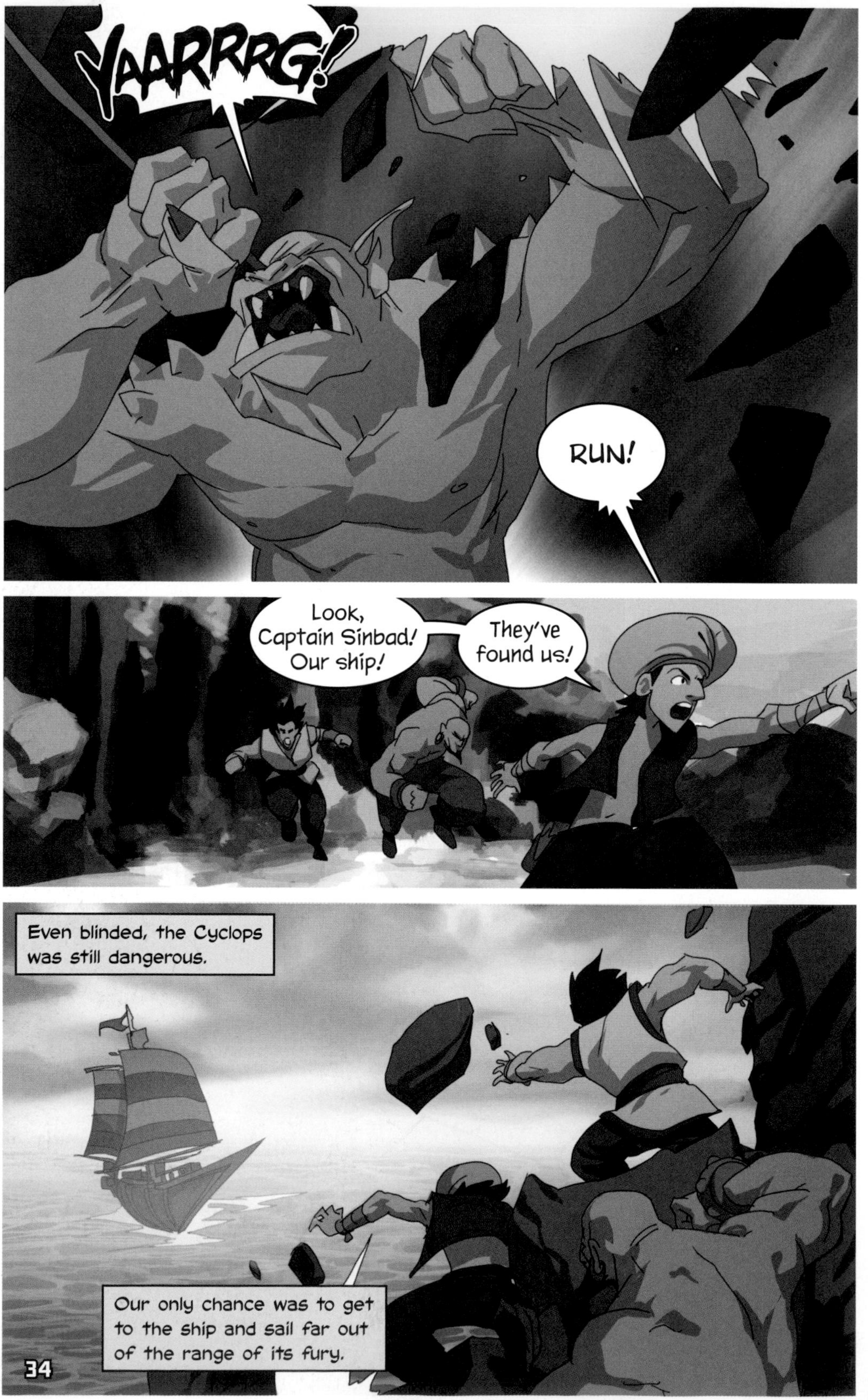
YAARRRG!
RUN!
Look, Captain Sinbad! Our ship!
They've found us!
Even blinded, the Cyclops was still dangerous.
Our only chance was to get to the ship and sail far out of the range of its fury.

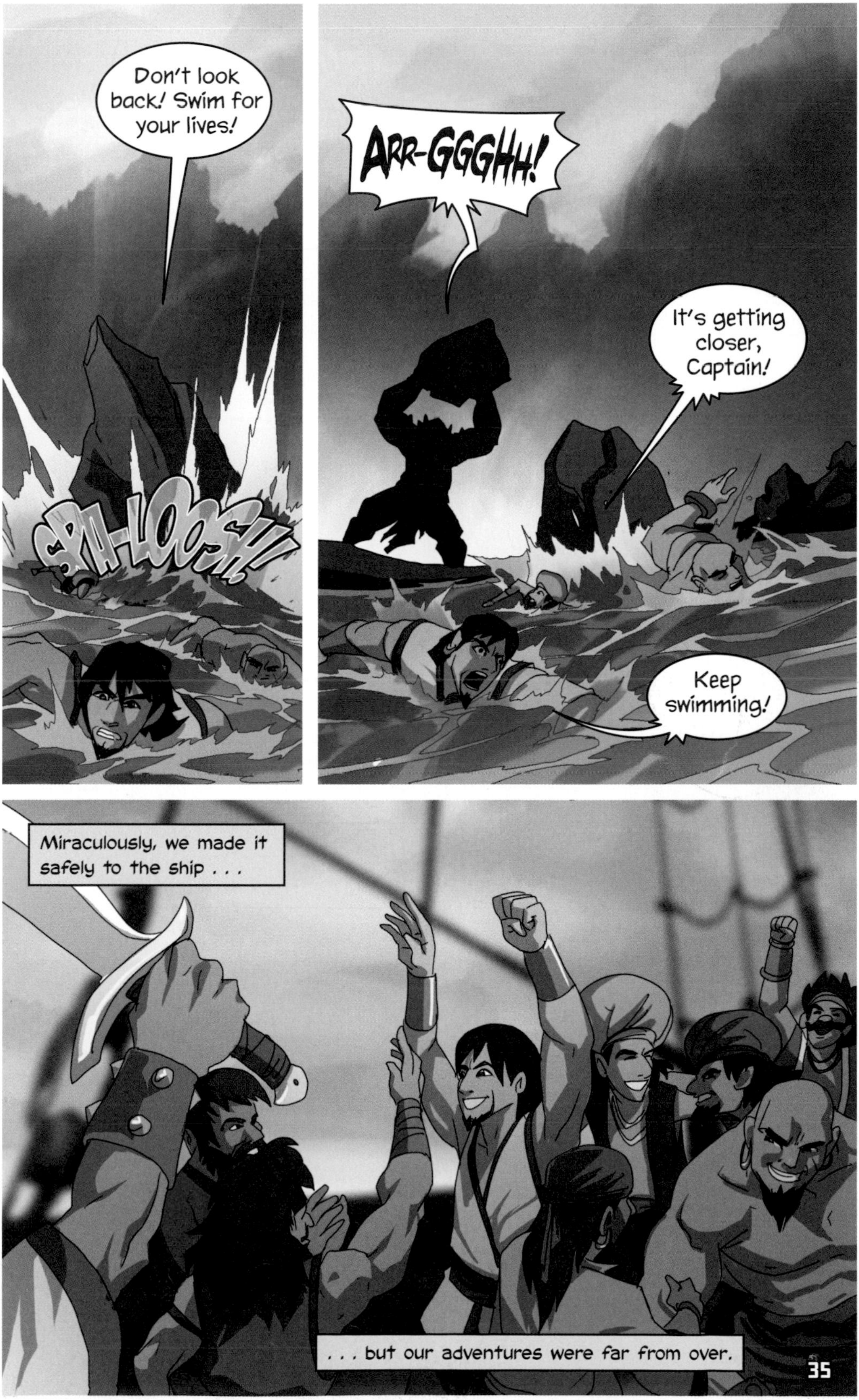
Don't look back! Swim for your lives!
SPA-LOOSH!
ARR-GGGHH!
It's getting closer, Captain!
Keep swimming!
Miraculously, we made it safely to the ship . . .
. . . but our adventures were far from over.

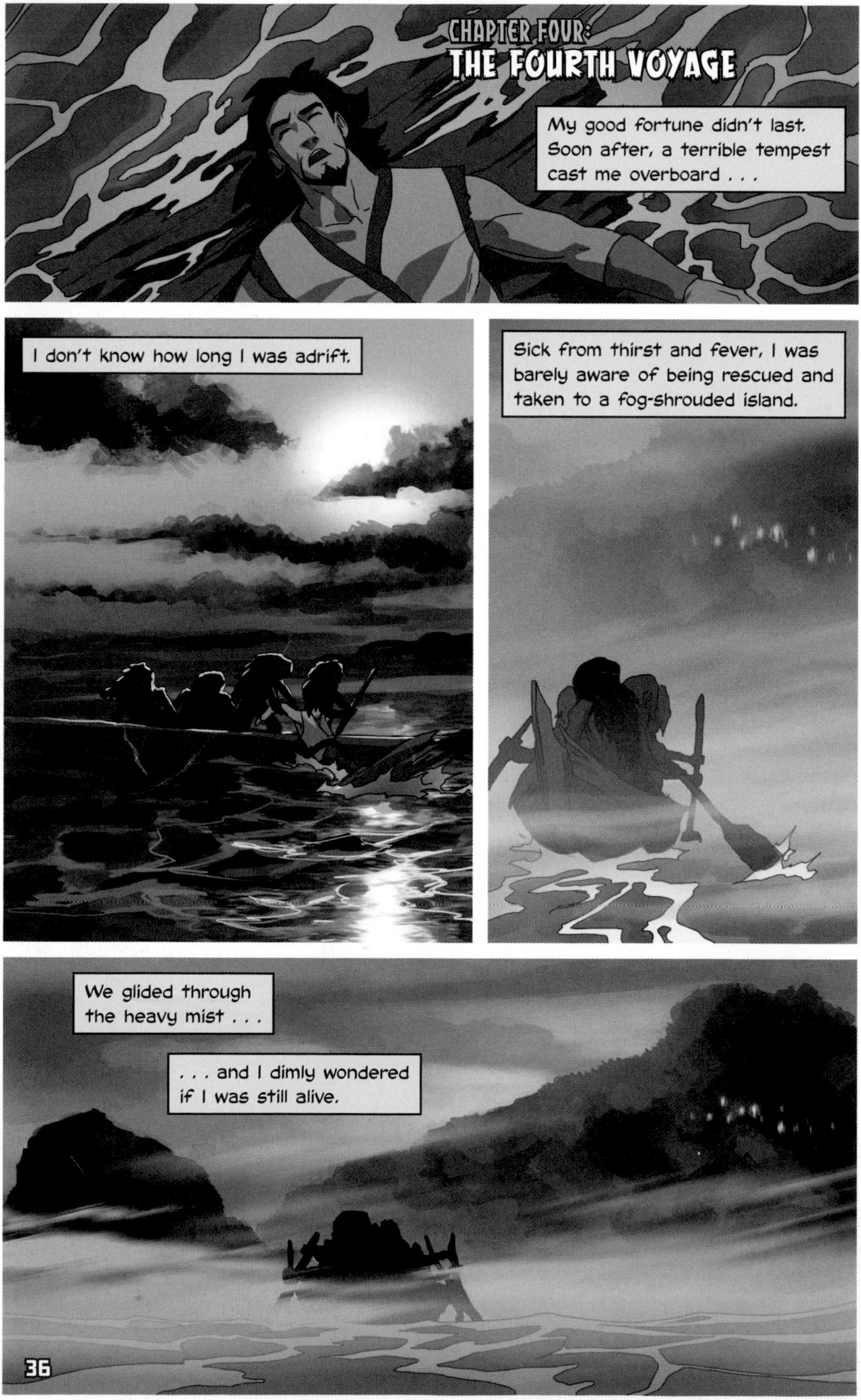
CHAPTER FOUR:
THE FOURTH VOYAGE
My good fortune didn't last. Soon after, a terrible tempest cast me overboard . . .
I don't know how long I was adrift.
Sick from thirst and fever, I was barely aware of being rescued and taken to a fog-shrouded island.
We glided through the heavy mist . . .
. . . and I dimly wondered if I was still alive.

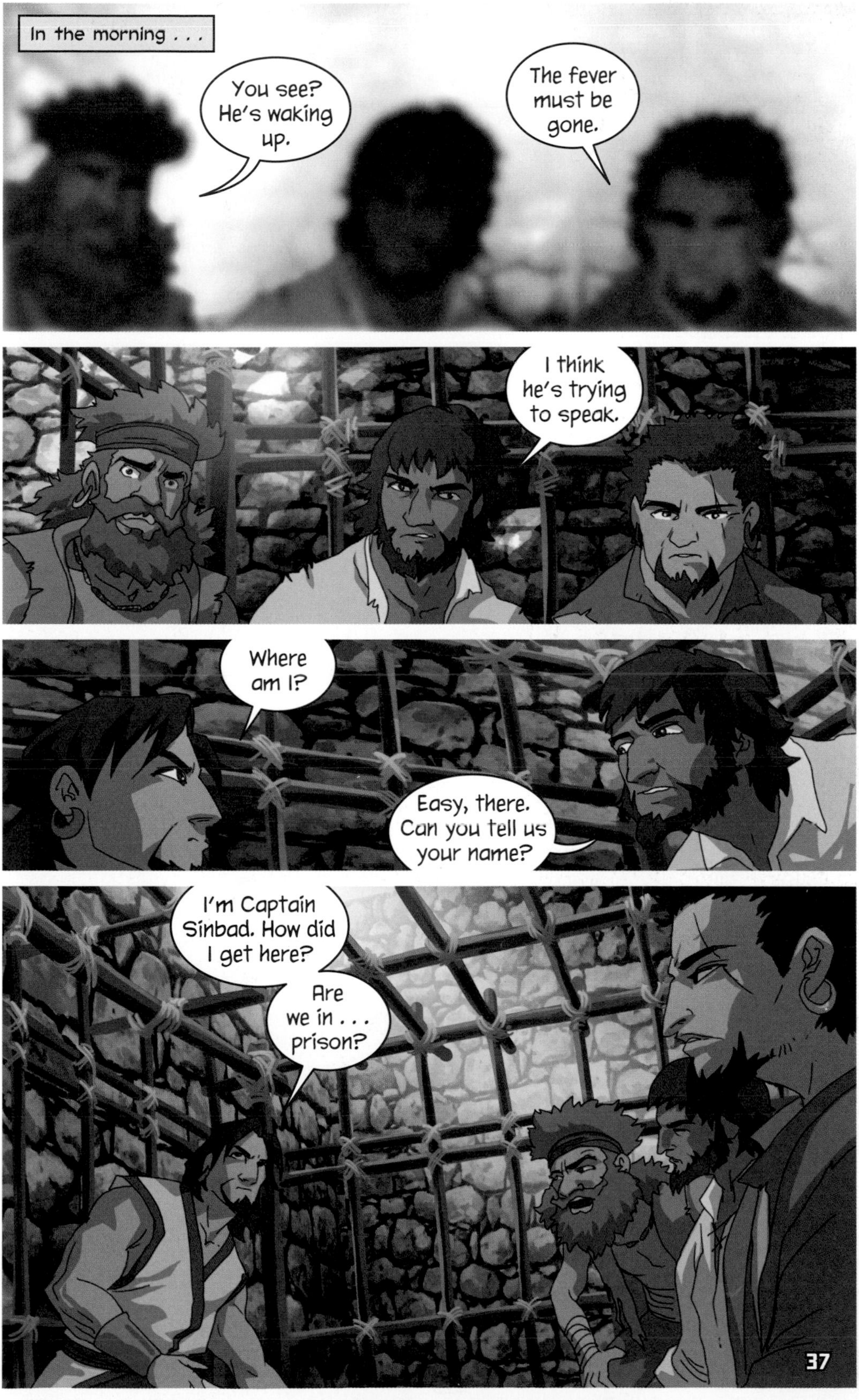
In the morning . . .
You see? He's waking up.
The fever must be gone.
I think he's trying to speak.
Where am I?
Easy, there. Can you tell us your name?
I'm Captain Sinbad. How did I get here?
Are we in . . . prison?

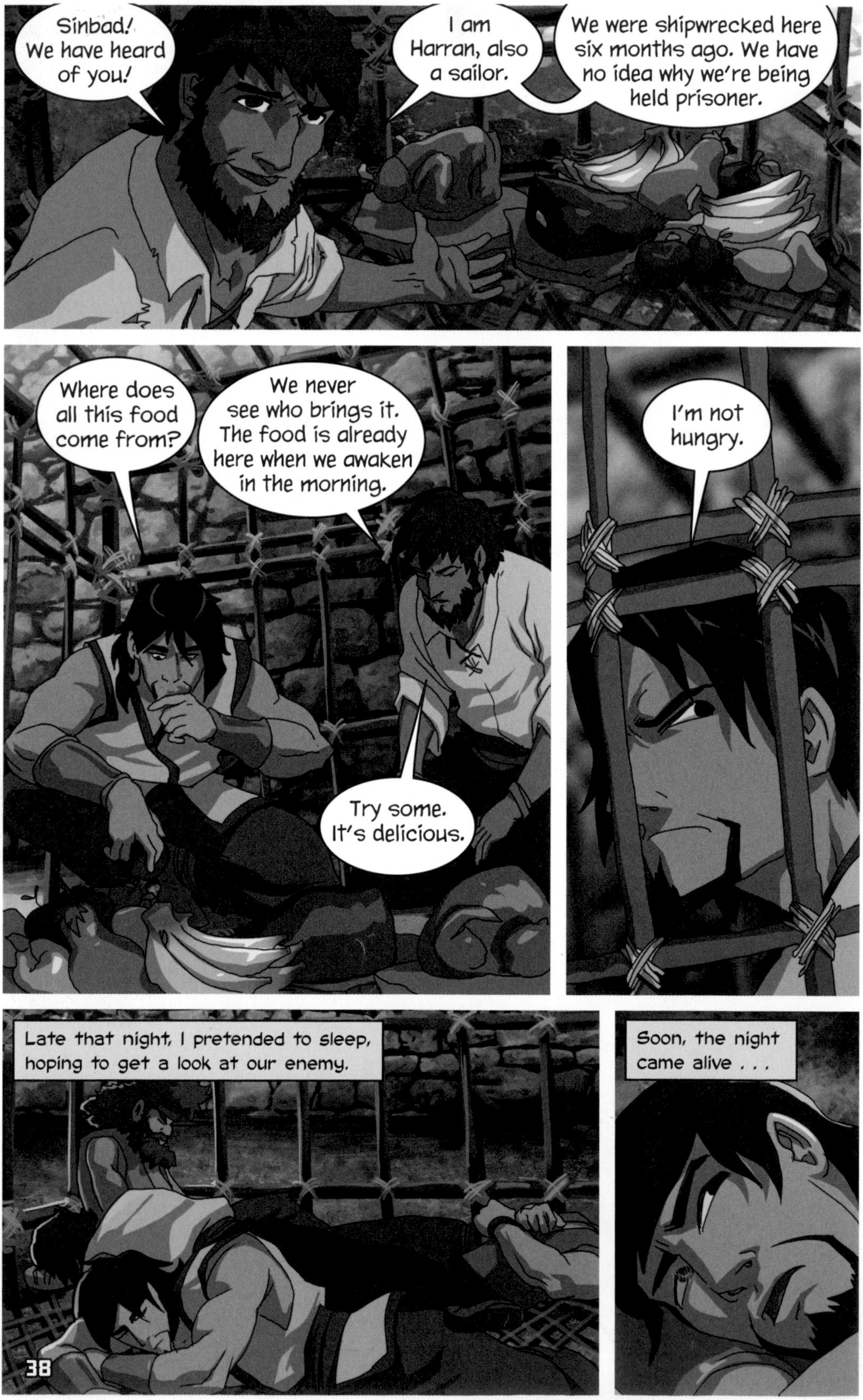
Sinbad! We have heard of you!
I am Harran, also a sailor.
We were shipwrecked here six months ago. We have no idea why we're being held prisoner.
Where does all this food come from?
We never see who brings it. The food is already here when we awaken in the morning.
Try some. It's delicious.
I'm not hungry.
Late that night, I pretended to sleep, hoping to get a look at our enemy.
Soon, the night came alive . . .

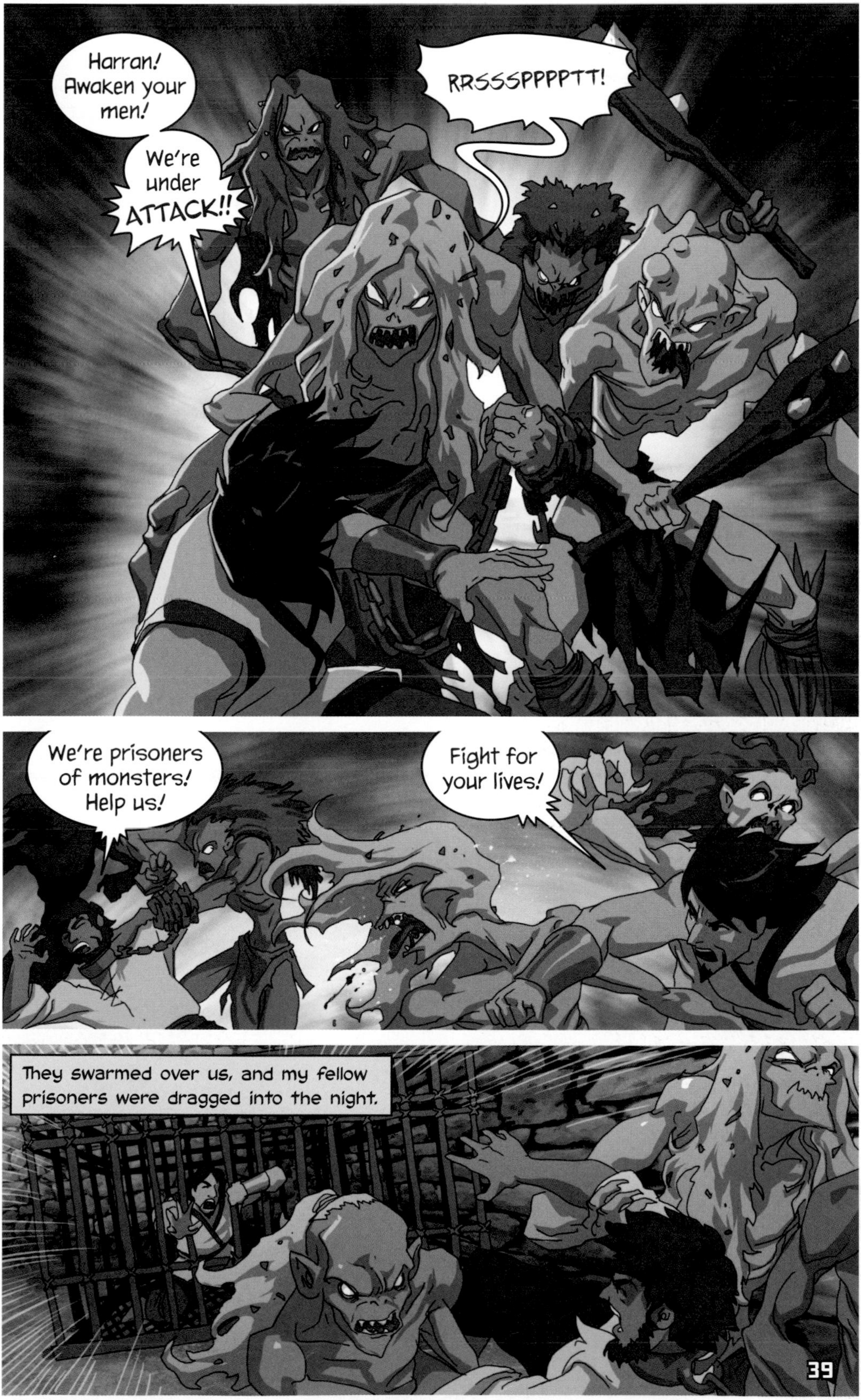
Harran! Awaken your men!
We're under ATTACK!!
RRSSSPPPPTT!
We're prisoners of monsters! Help us!
Fight for your lives!
They swarmed over us, and my fellow prisoners were dragged into the night.
39

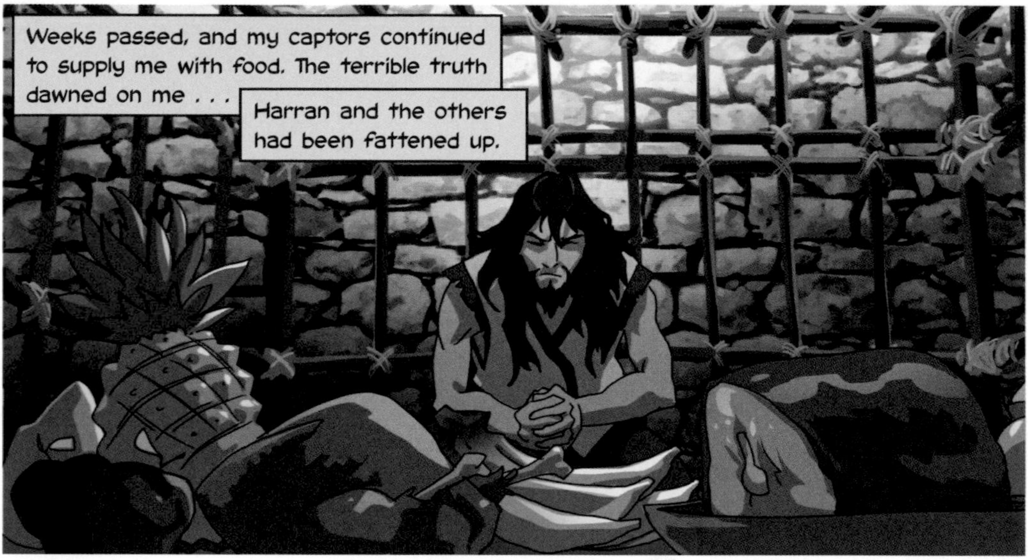
Weeks passed, and my captors continued to supply me with food. The terrible truth dawned on me . . .
Harran and the others had been fattened up.

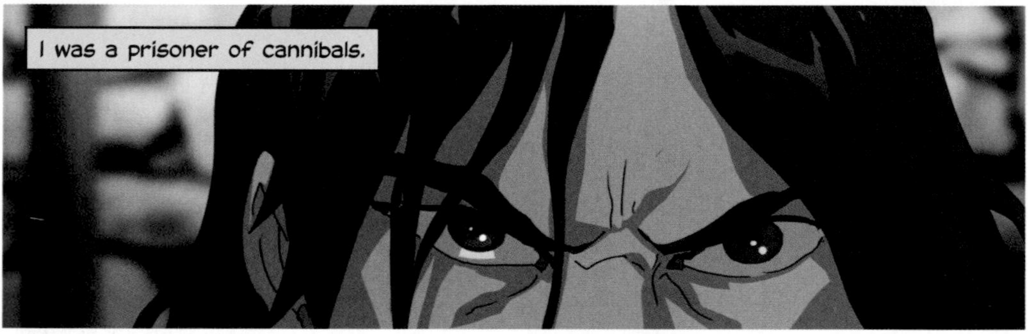
I was a prisoner of cannibals.

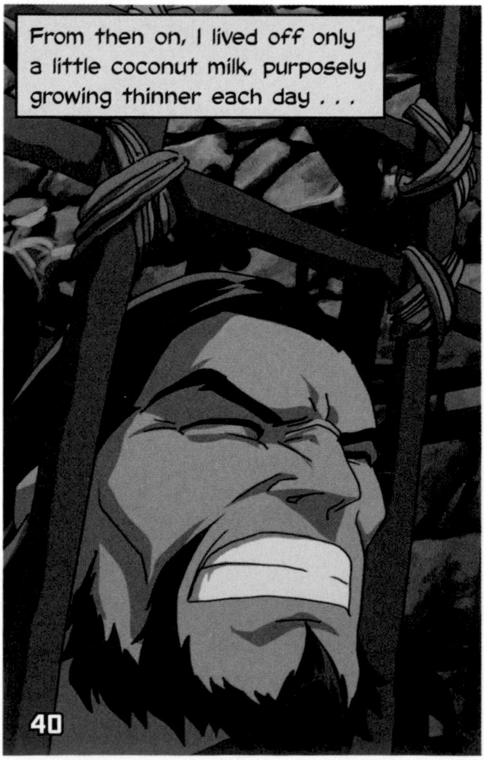
From then on, I lived off only a little coconut milk, purposely growing thinner each day . . .

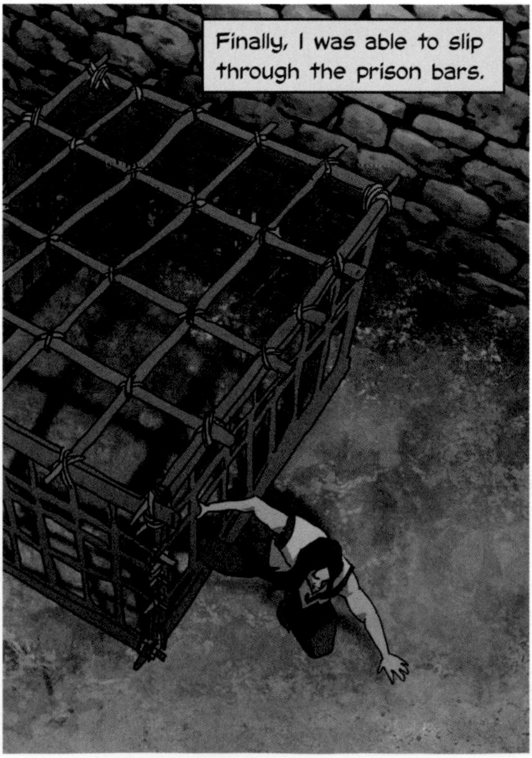
Finally, I was able to slip through the prison bars.

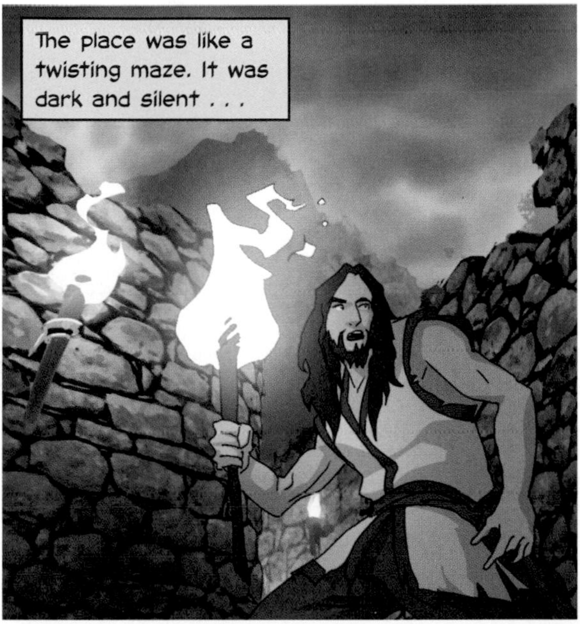
The place was like a twisting maze. It was dark and silent . . .

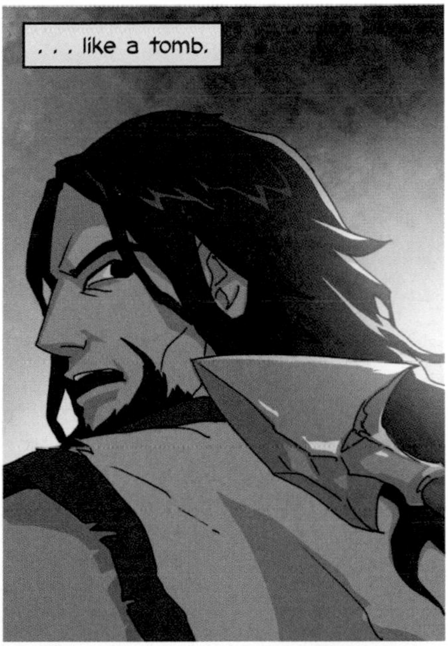
. . . like a tomb.

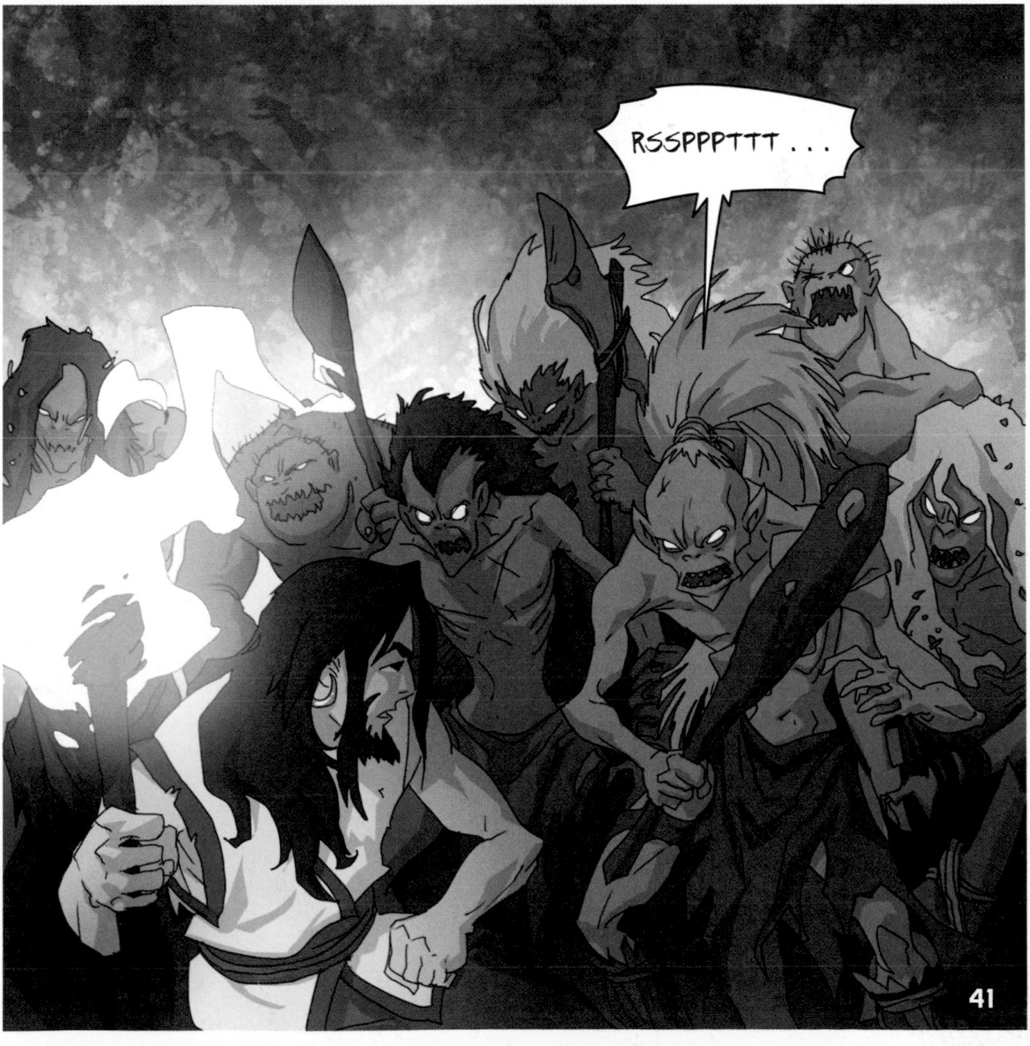
RSSPPPTTT . . .

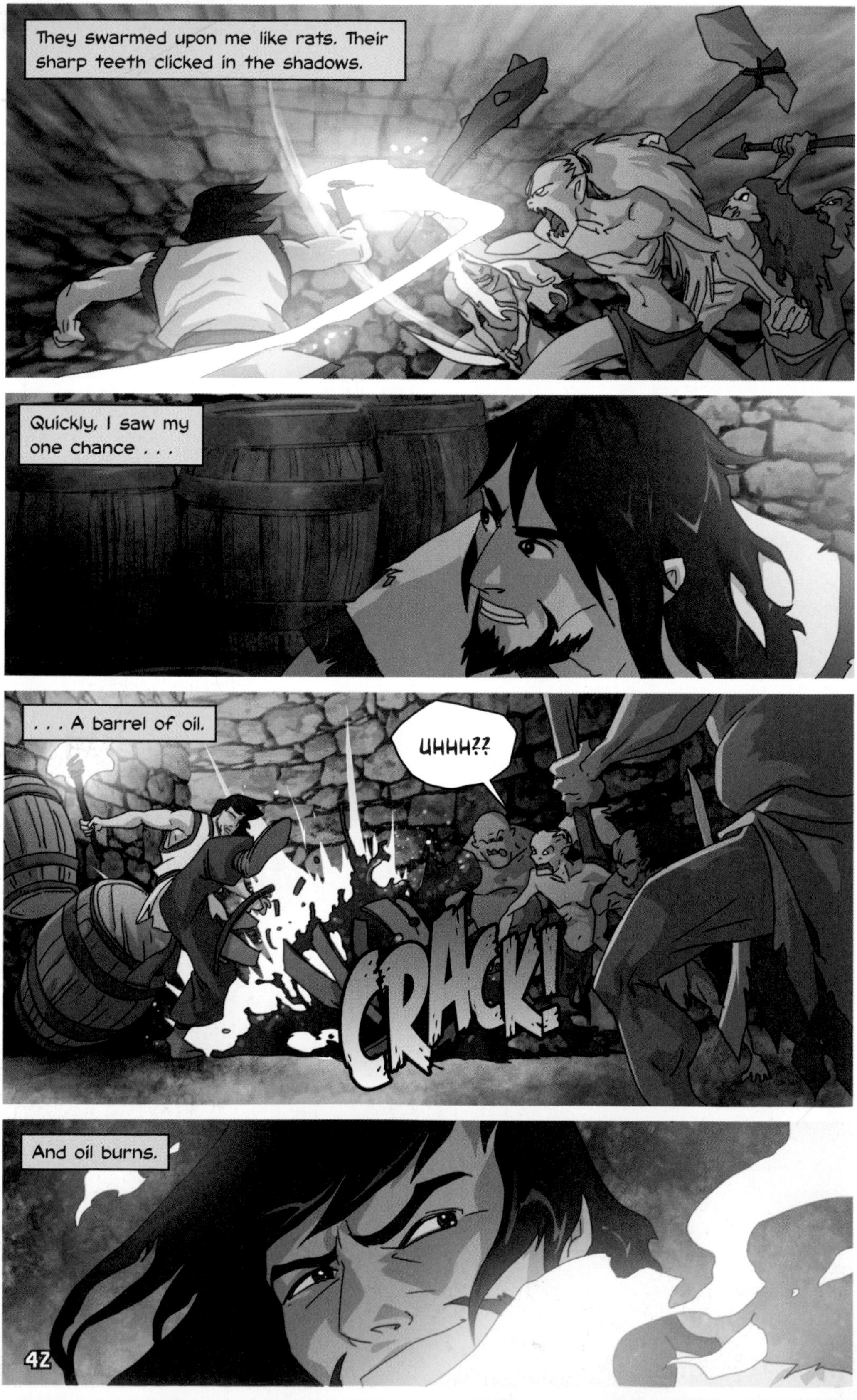
They swarmed upon me like rats. Their sharp teeth clicked in the shadows.
Quickly, I saw my one chance . . .
. . . A barrel of oil.
UHHH??
CRACK!
And oil burns.

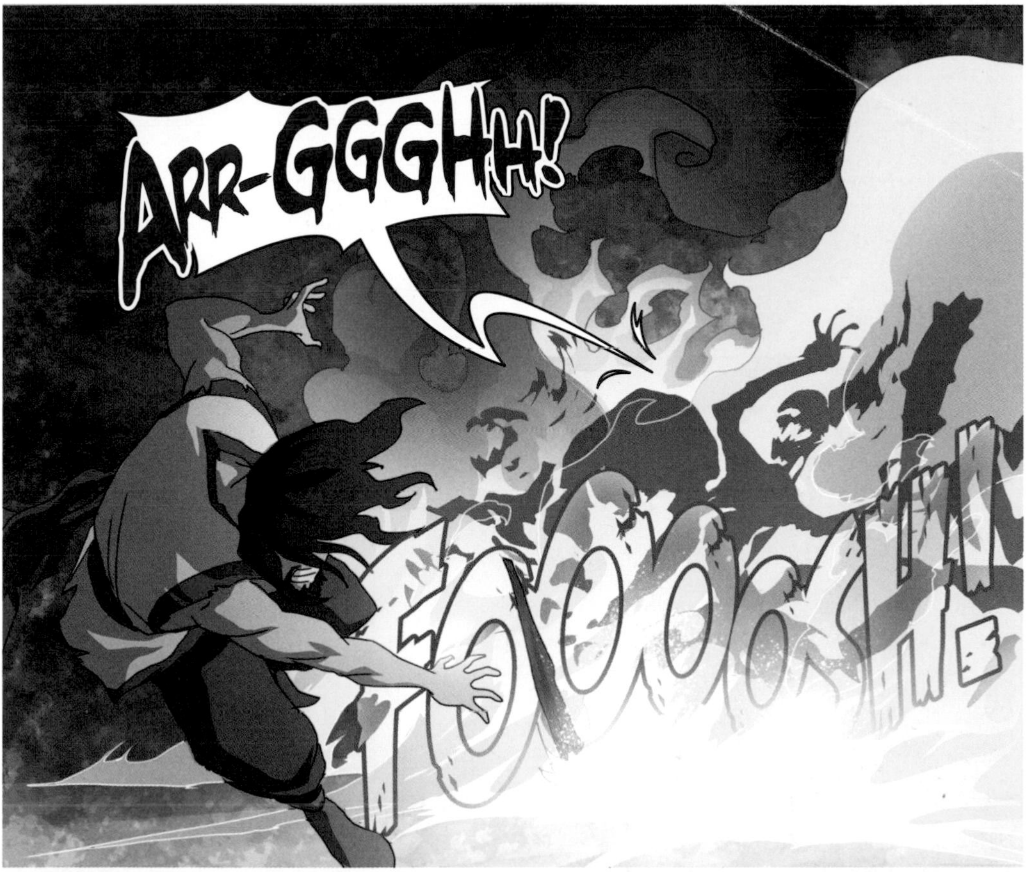
ARR-GGGHH!
FOOOOSH!

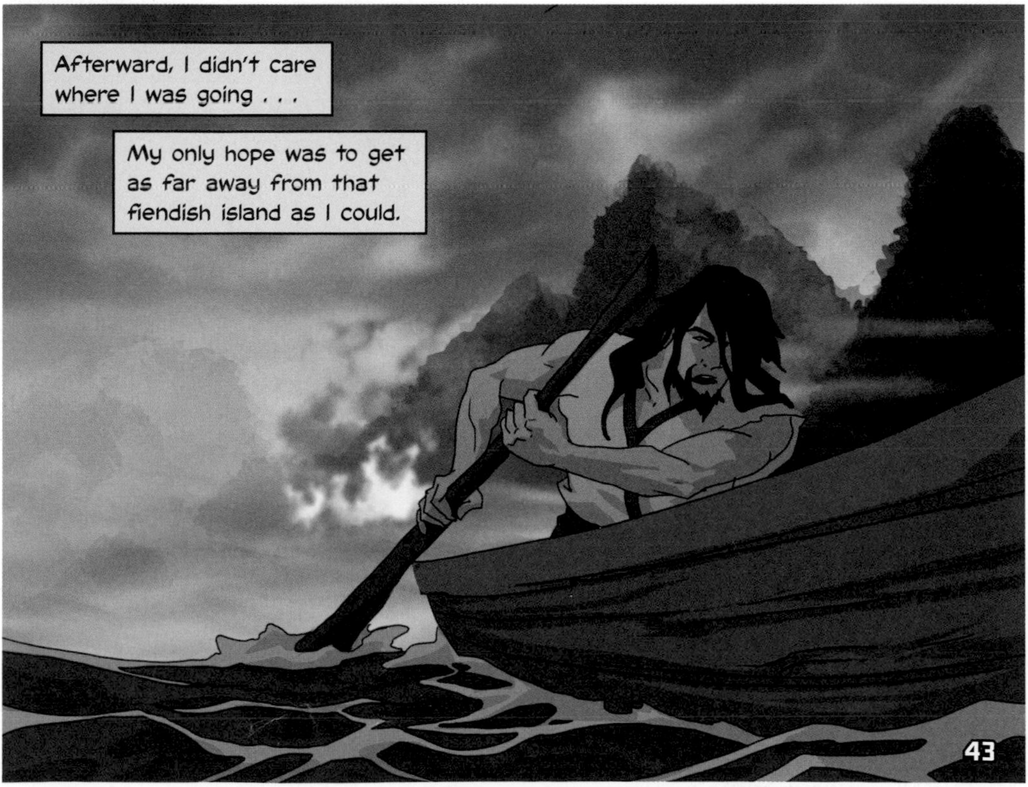
Afterward, I didn't care where I was going . . .
My only hope was to get as far away from that fiendish island as I could.

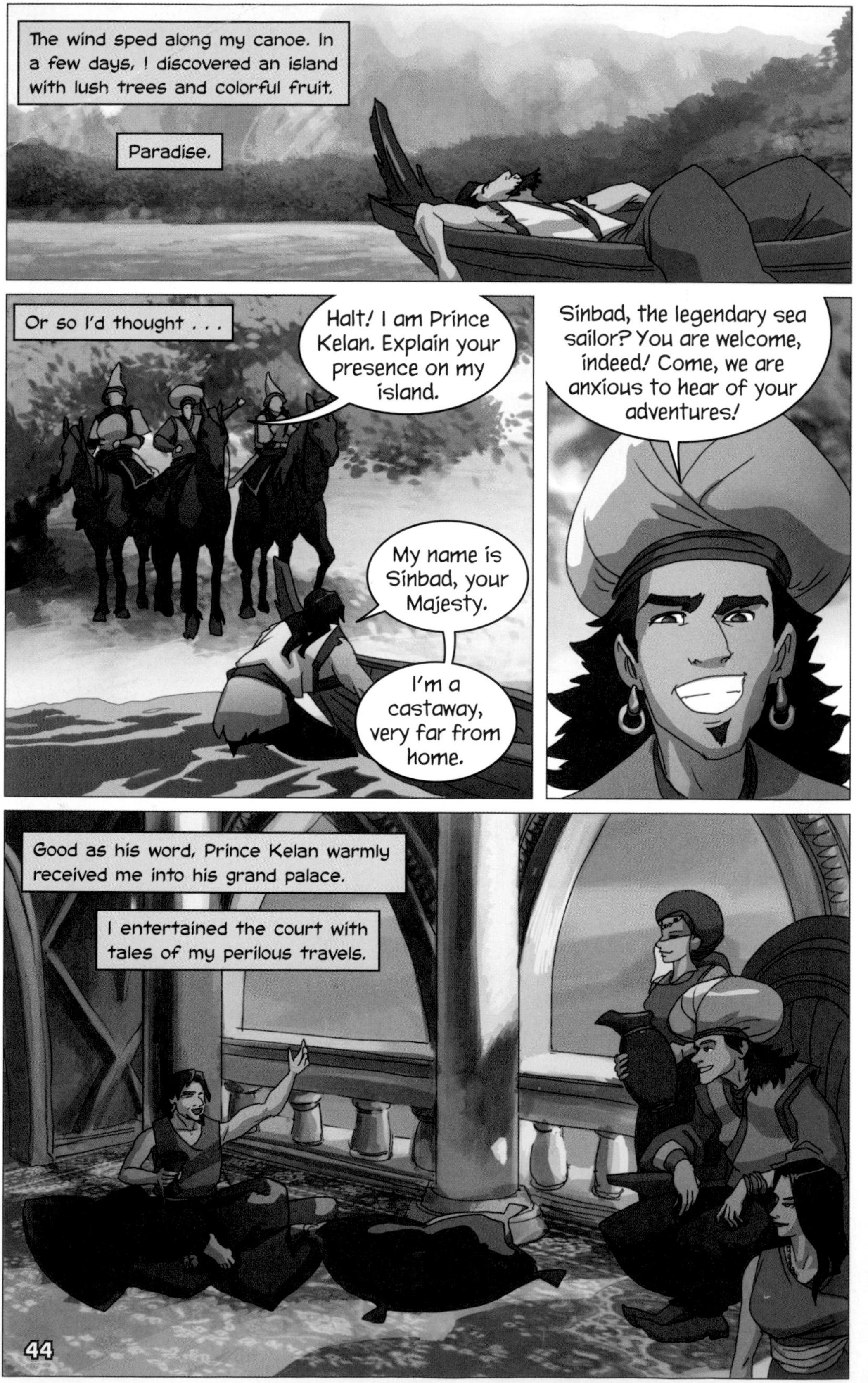
The wind sped along my canoe. In a few days, I discovered an island with lush trees and colorful fruit.
Paradise.
Or so I'd thought . . .
Halt! I am Prince Kelan. Explain your presence on my island.
My name is Sinbad, your Majesty.
I'm a castaway, very far from home.
Sinbad, the legendary sea sailor? You are welcome, indeed! Come, we are anxious to hear of your adventures!
Good as his word, Prince Kelan warmly received me into his grand palace.
I entertained the court with tales of my perilous travels.

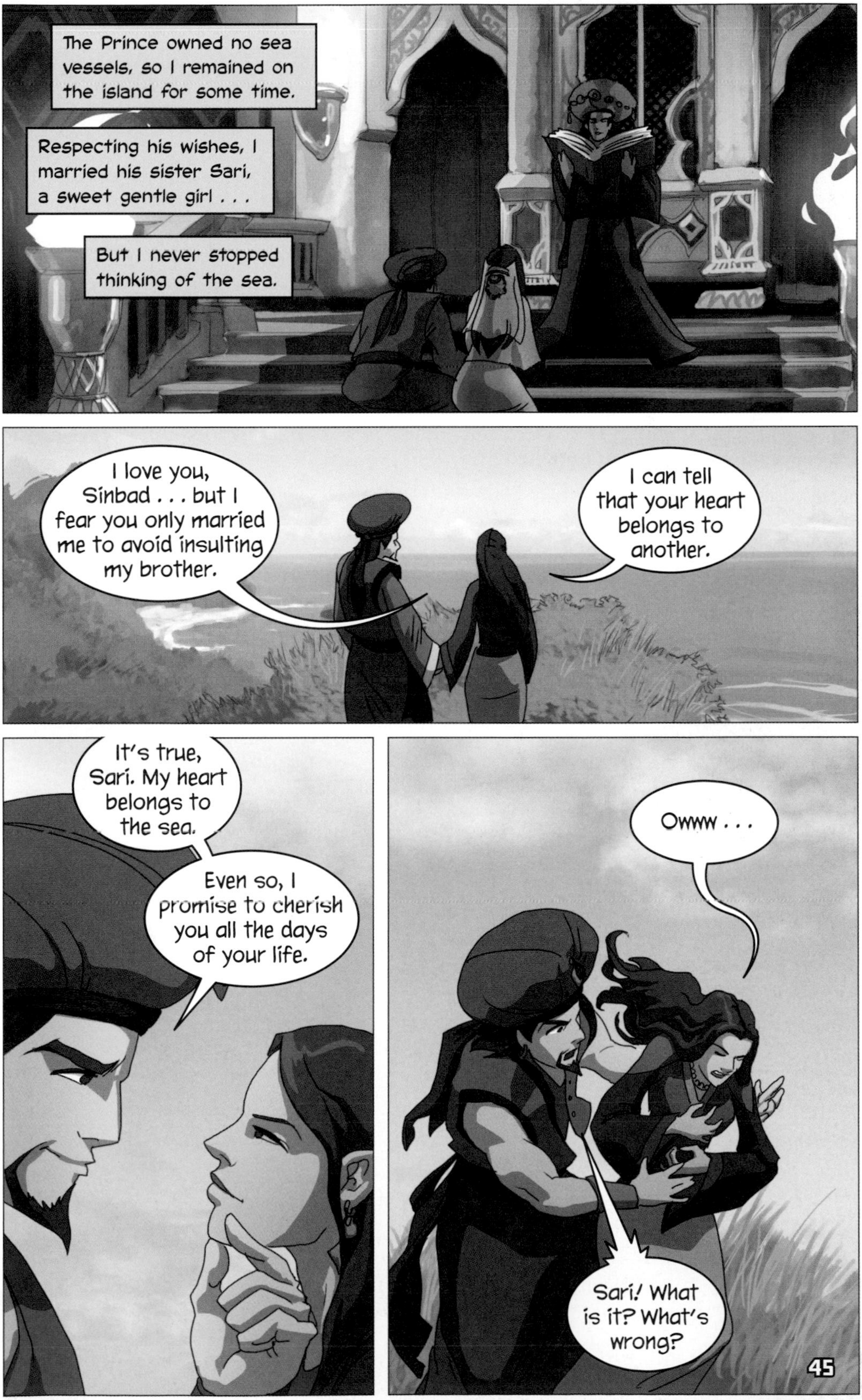
The Prince owned no sea vessels, so I remained on the island for some time.
Respecting his wishes, I married his sister Sari, a sweet gentle girl . . .
But I never stopped thinking of the sea.
I love you, Sinbad . . . but I fear you only married me to avoid insulting my brother.
I can tell that your heart belongs to another.
It's true, Sari. My heart belongs to the sea.
Even so, I promise to cherish you all the days of your life.
Owww . . .
Sari! What is it? What's wrong?

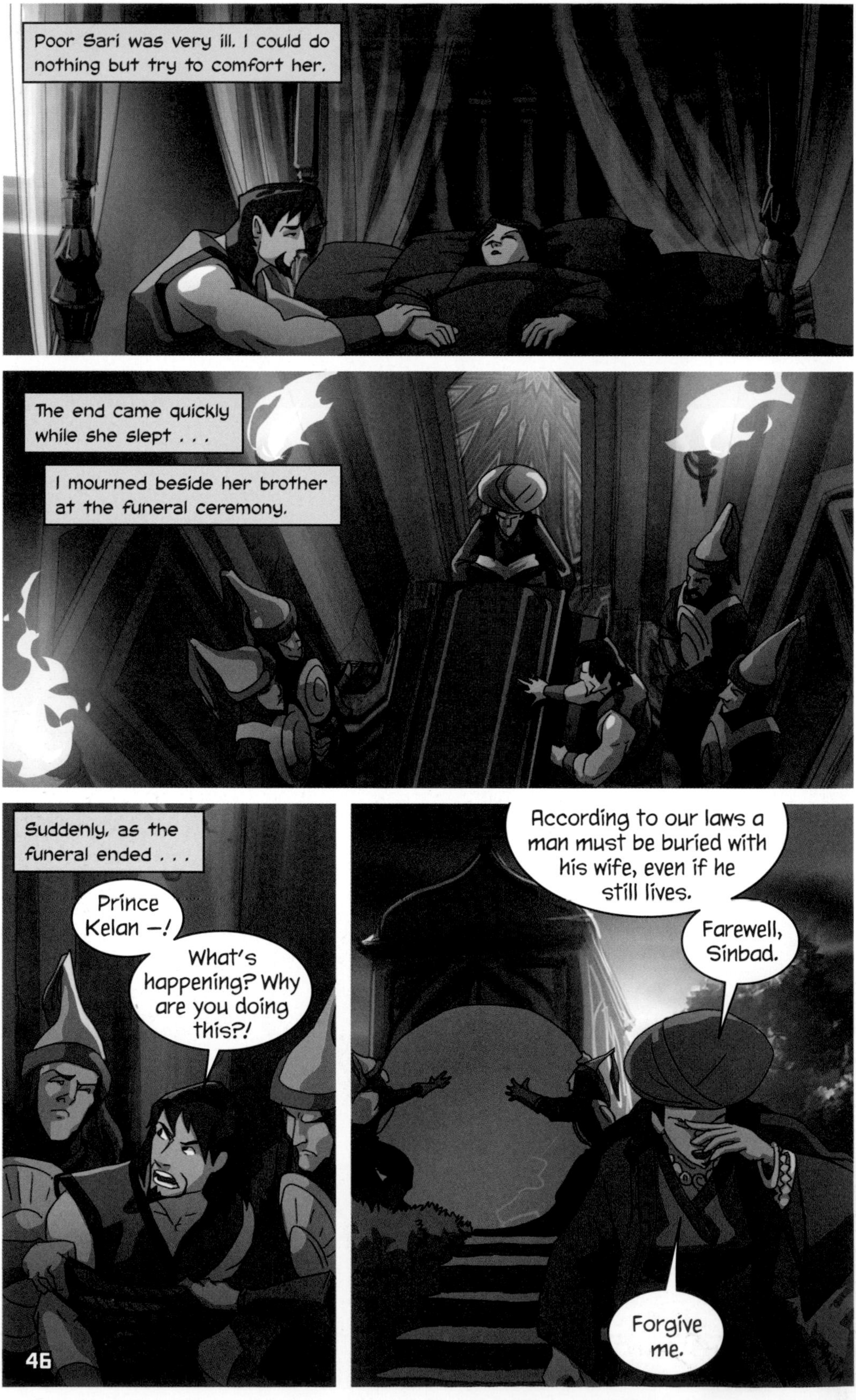
Poor Sari was very ill. I could do nothing but try to comfort her.
The end came quickly while she slept . . .
I mourned beside her brother at the funeral ceremony.
Suddenly, as the funeral ended . . .
Prince Kelan –!
What's happening? Why are you doing this?!
According to our laws a man must be buried with his wife, even if he still lives.
Farewell, Sinbad.
Forgive me.

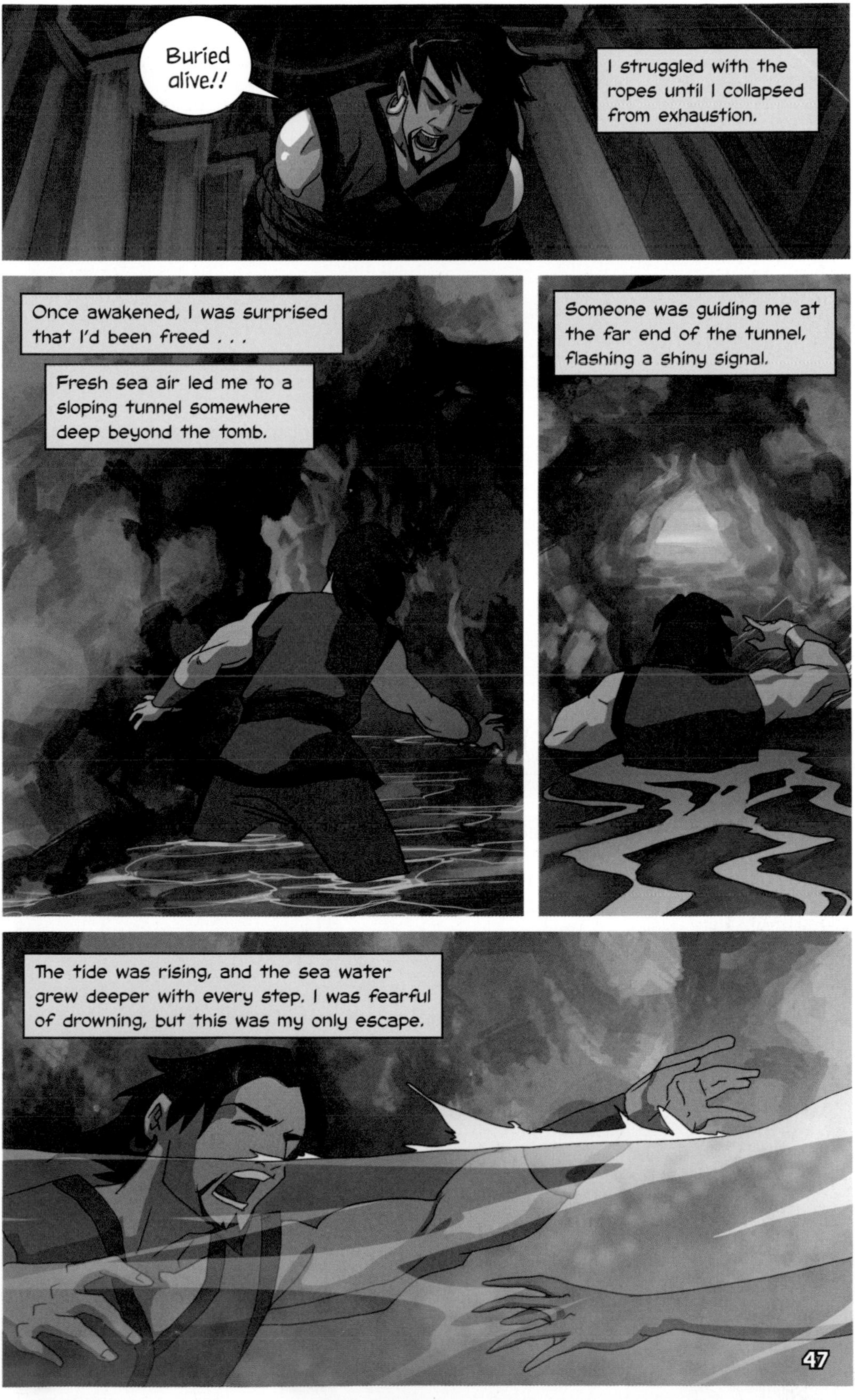
Buried alive!!
I struggled with the ropes until I collapsed from exhaustion.
Once awakened, I was surprised that I'd been freed . . .
Fresh sea air led me to a sloping tunnel somewhere deep beyond the tomb.
Someone was guiding me at the far end of the tunnel, flashing a shiny signal.
The tide was rising, and the sea water grew deeper with every step. I was fearful of drowning, but this was my only escape.

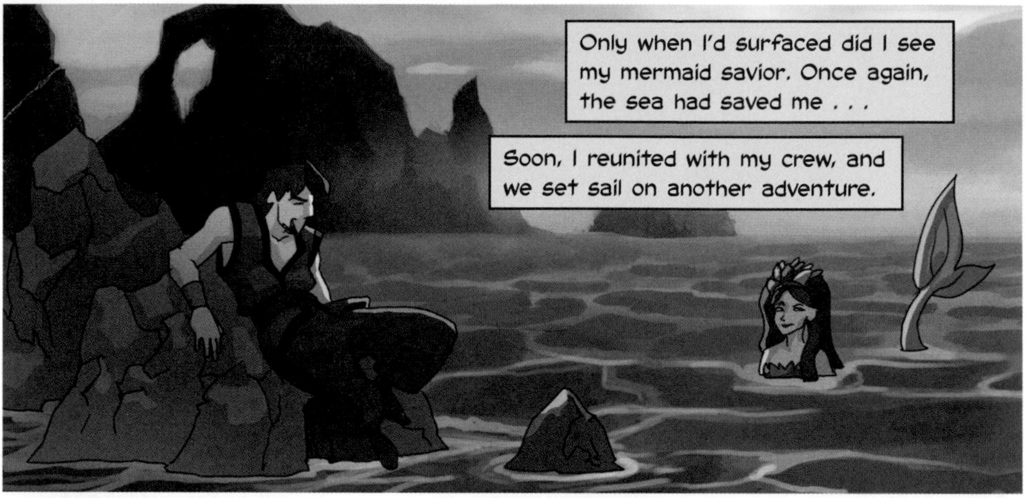
Only when I'd surfaced did I see my mermaid savior. Once again, the sea had saved me . . .
Soon, I reunited with my crew, and we set sail on another adventure.

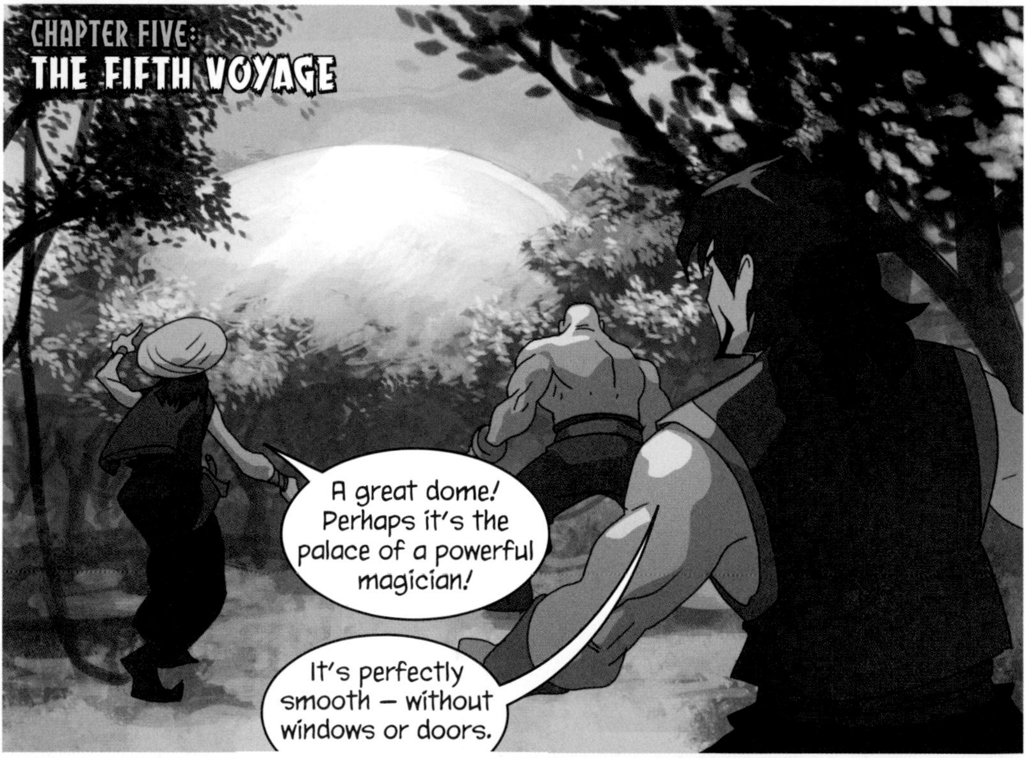
CHAPTER FIVE:
THE FIFTH VOYAGE
A great dome! Perhaps it's the palace of a powerful magician!
It's perfectly smooth — without windows or doors.

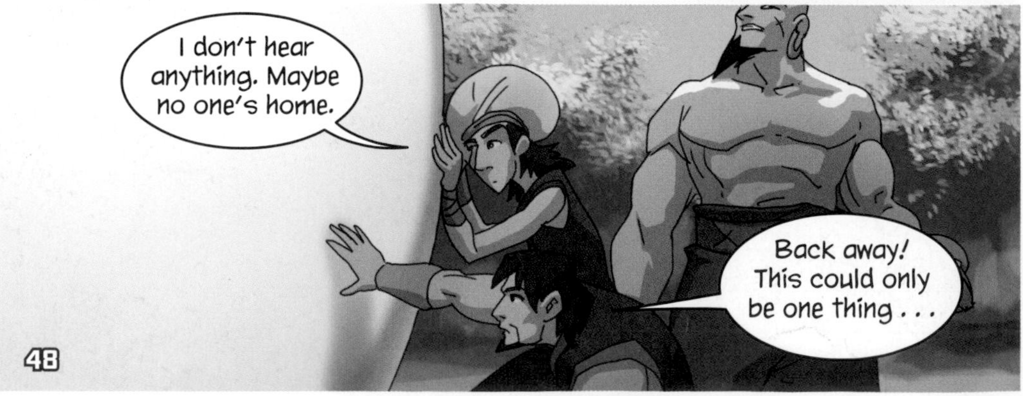
I don't hear anything. Maybe no one's home.
Back away! This could only be one thing . . .

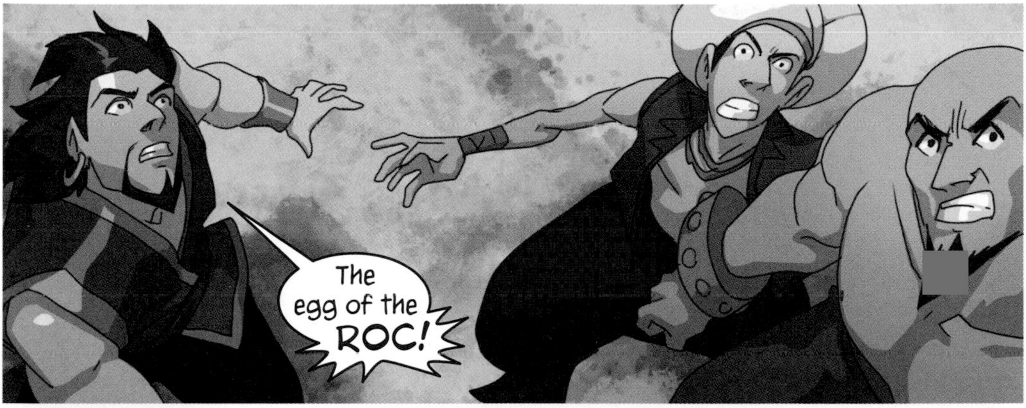
The egg of the ROC!

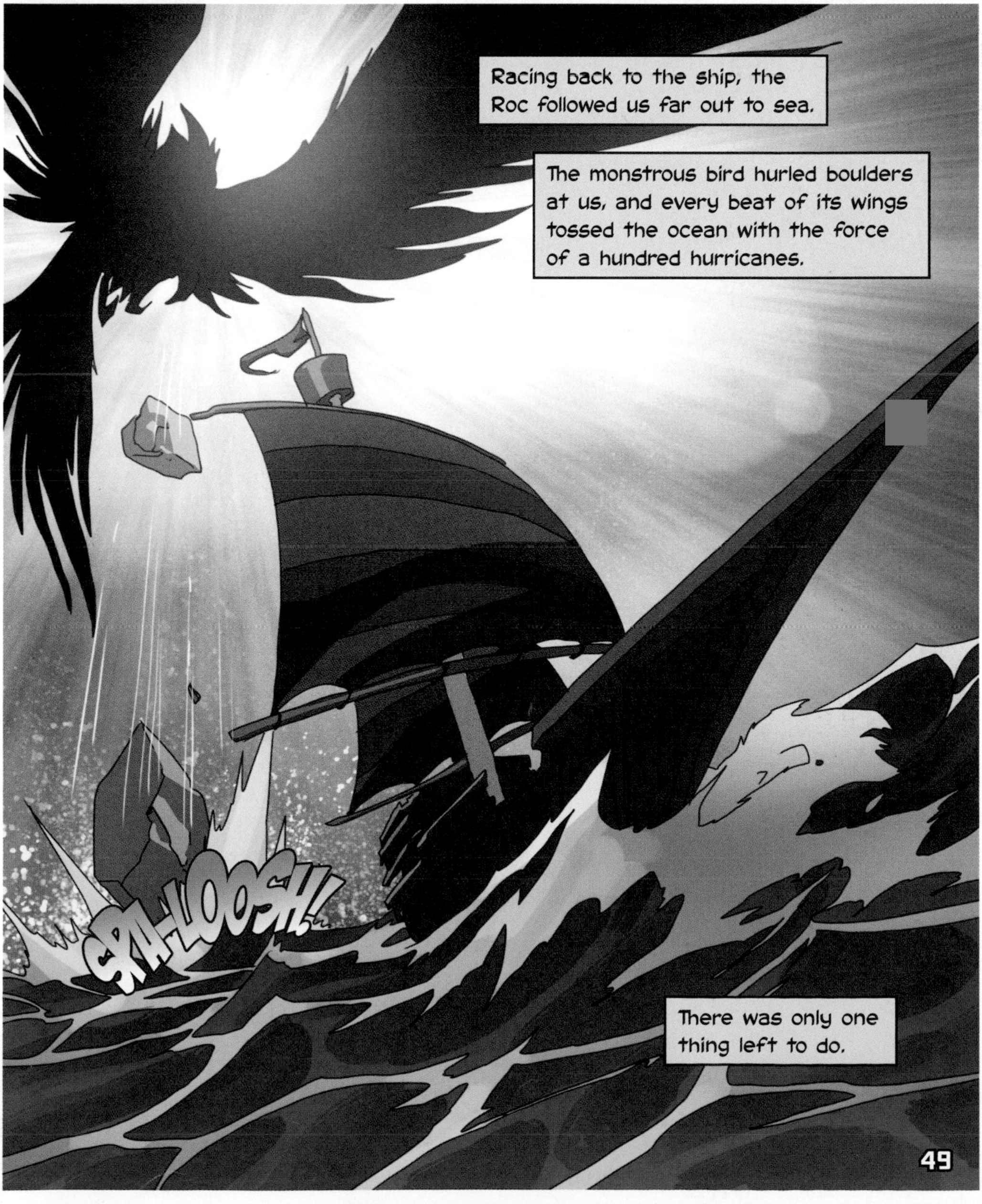
Racing back to the ship, the Roc followed us far out to sea.
The monstrous bird hurled boulders at us, and every beat of its wings tossed the ocean with the force of a hundred hurricanes.
SPA-LOOSH!
There was only one thing left to do.

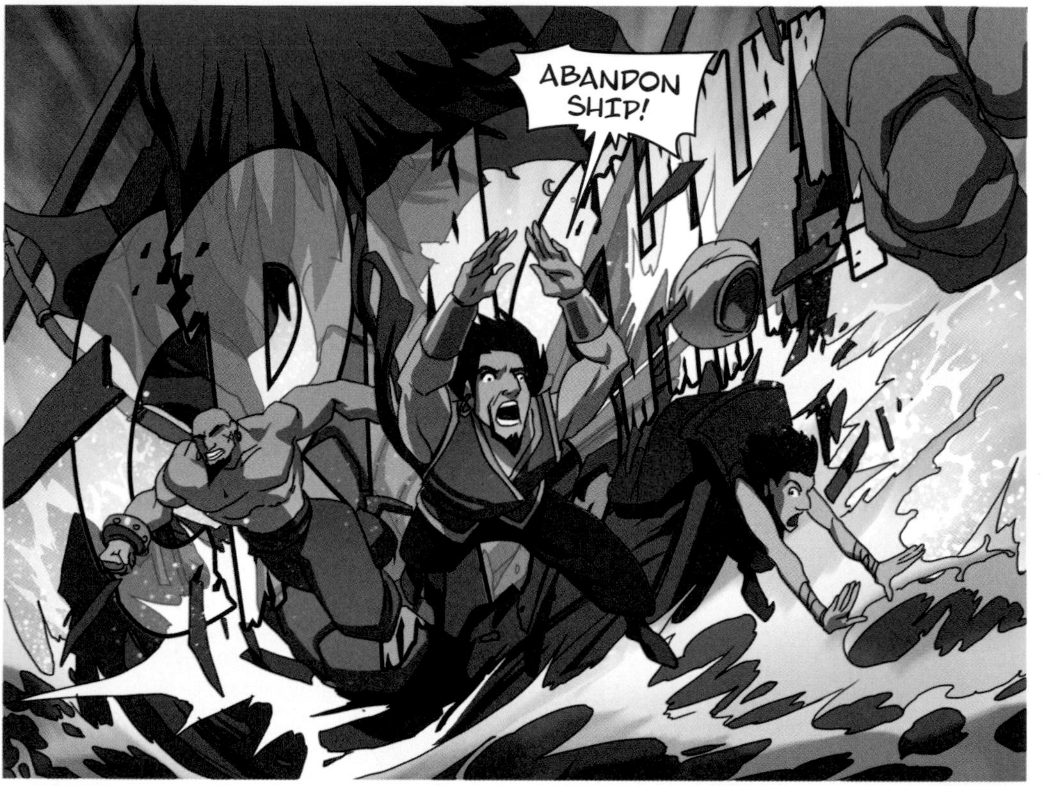
ABANDON SHIP!

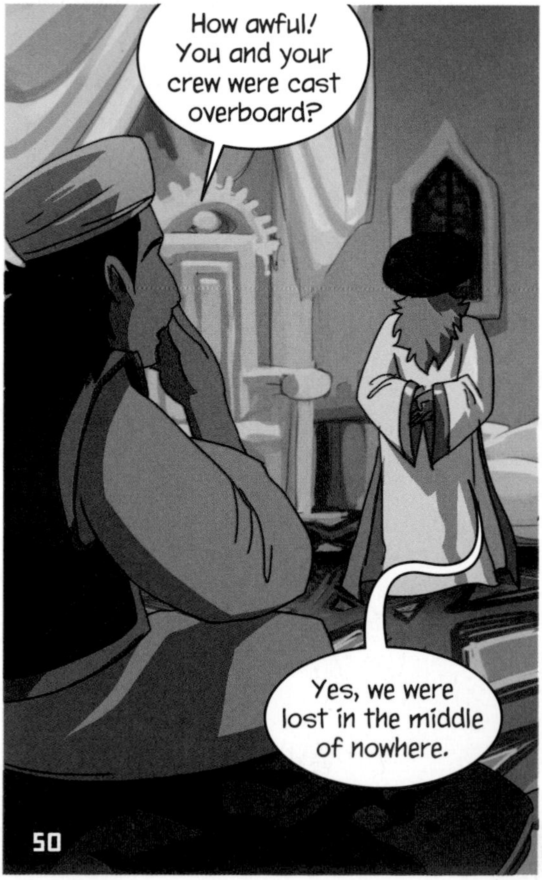
How awful! You and your crew were cast overboard?
Yes, we were lost in the middle of nowhere.

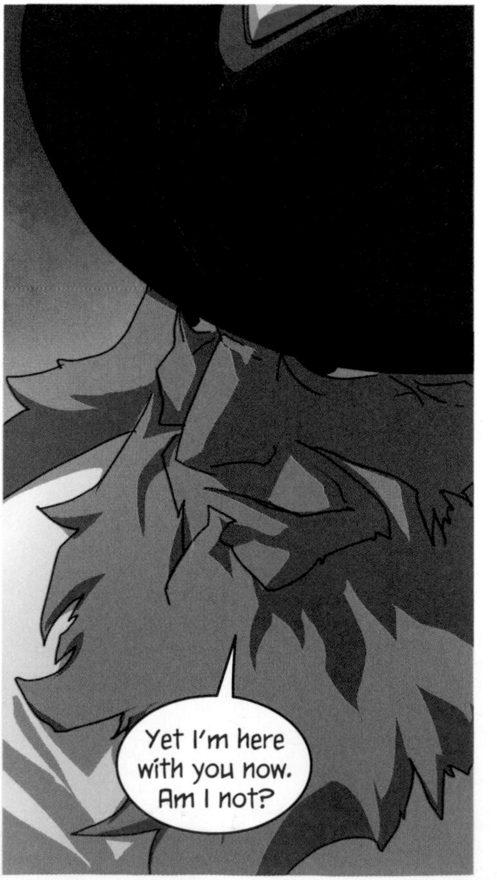
Yet I'm here with you now. Am I not?

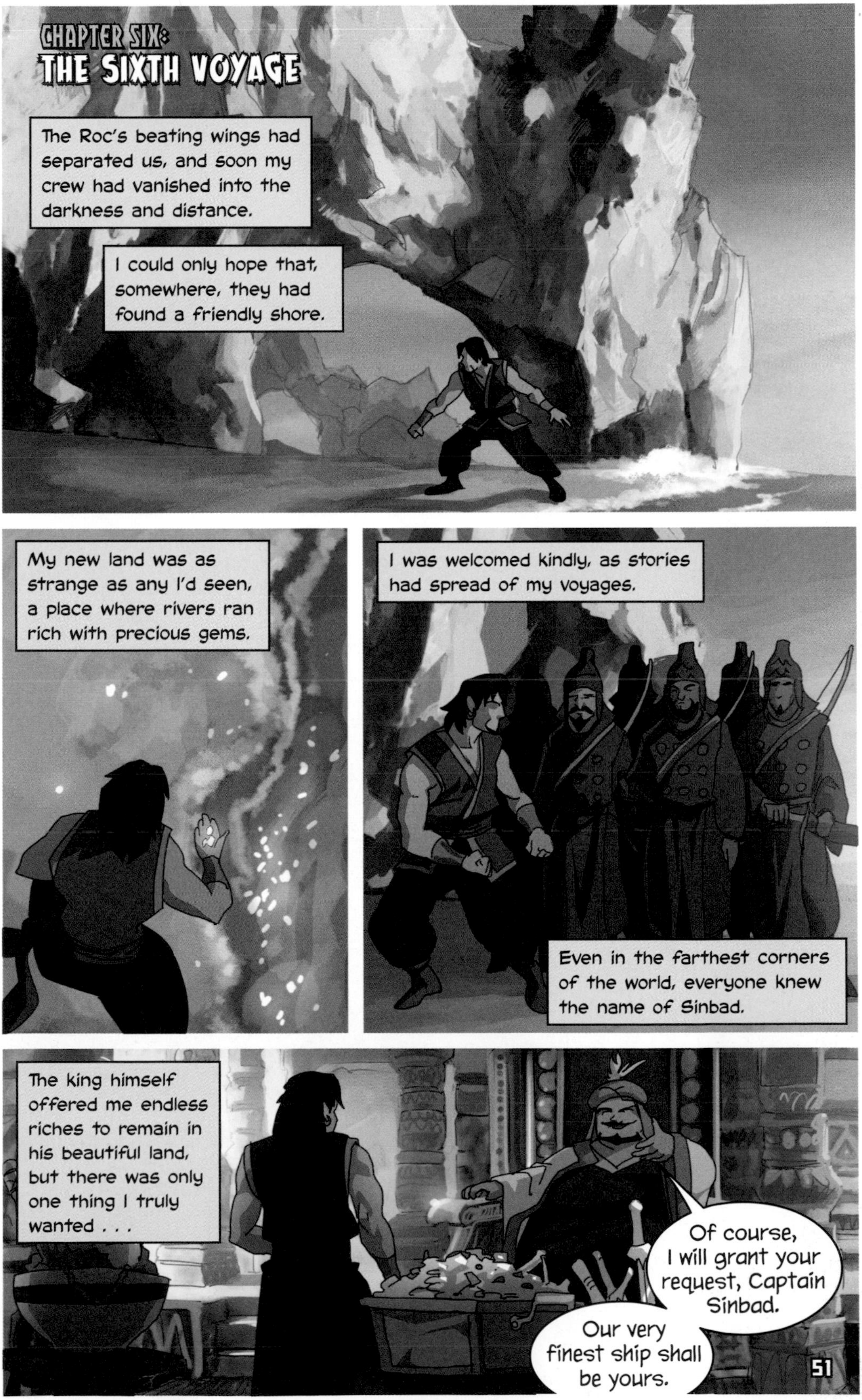
CHAPTER SIX:
THE SIXTH VOYAGE
The Roc's beating wings had separated us, and soon my crew had vanished into the darkness and distance.
I could only hope that, somewhere, they had found a friendly shore.
My new land was as strange as any I'd seen, a place where rivers ran rich with precious gems.
I was welcomed kindly, as stories had spread of my voyages.
Even in the farthest corners of the world, everyone knew the name of Sinbad.
The king himself offered me endless riches to remain in his beautiful land, but there was only one thing I truly wanted . . .
Of course, I will grant your request, Captain Sinbad.
Our very finest ship shall be yours.

CHAPTER SEVEN:
THE SEVENTH VOYAGE

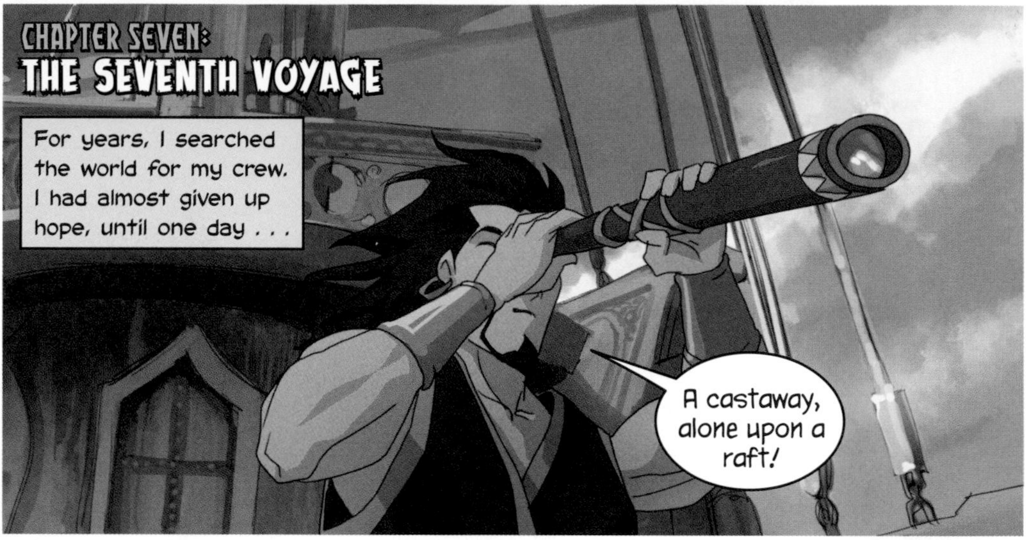

For years, I searched the world for my crew. I had almost given up hope, until one day . . .
A castaway, alone upon a raft!

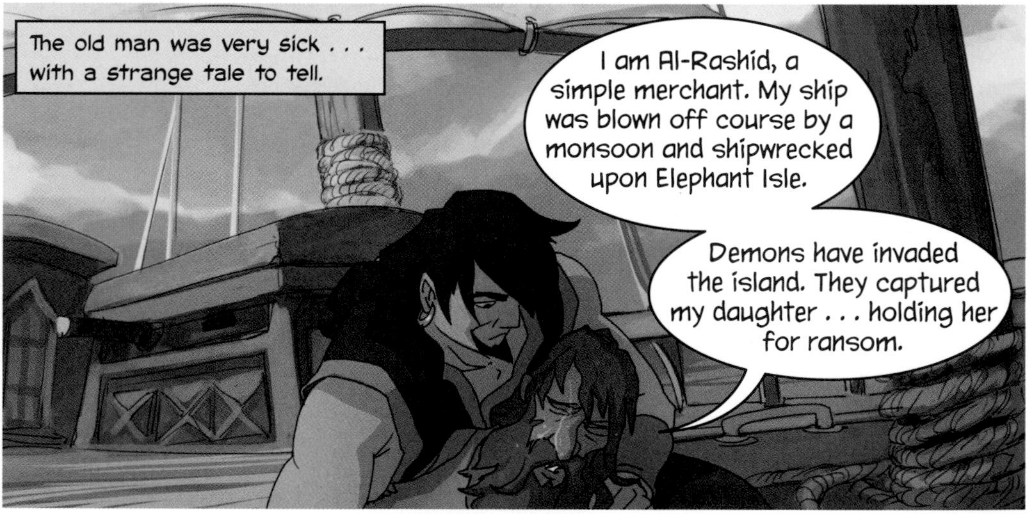

The old man was very sick . . . with a strange tale to tell.
I am Al-Rashid, a simple merchant. My ship was blown off course by a monsoon and shipwrecked upon Elephant Isle.
Demons have invaded the island. They captured my daughter . . . holding her for ransom.

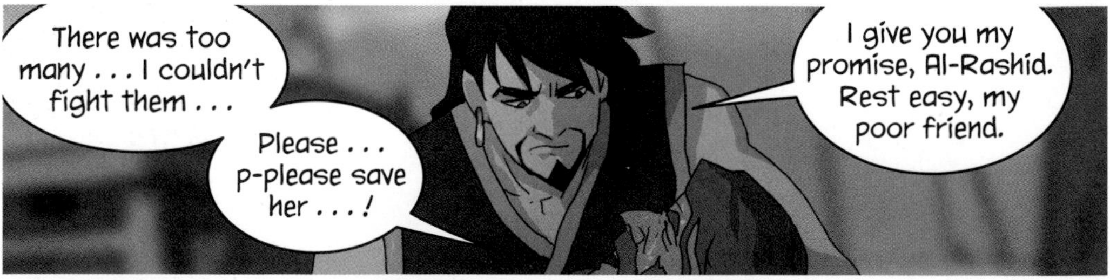

There was too many . . . I couldn't fight them . . .
Please . . . p-please save her . . . !
I give you my promise, Al-Rashid. Rest easy, my poor friend.

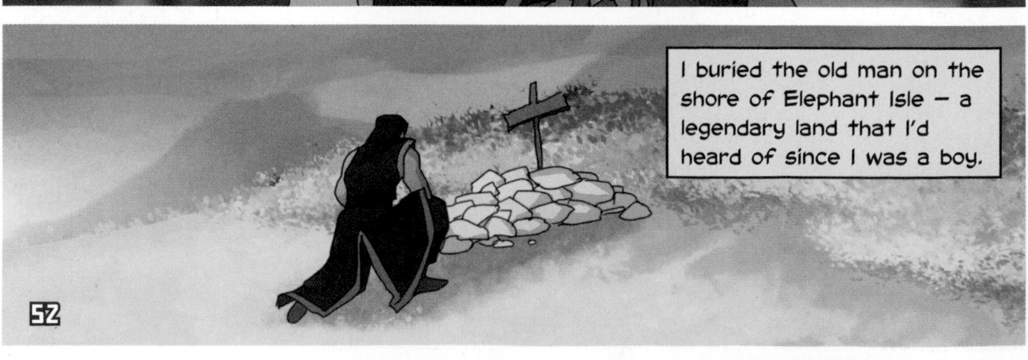

I buried the old man on the shore of Elephant Isle — a legendary land that I'd heard of since I was a boy.

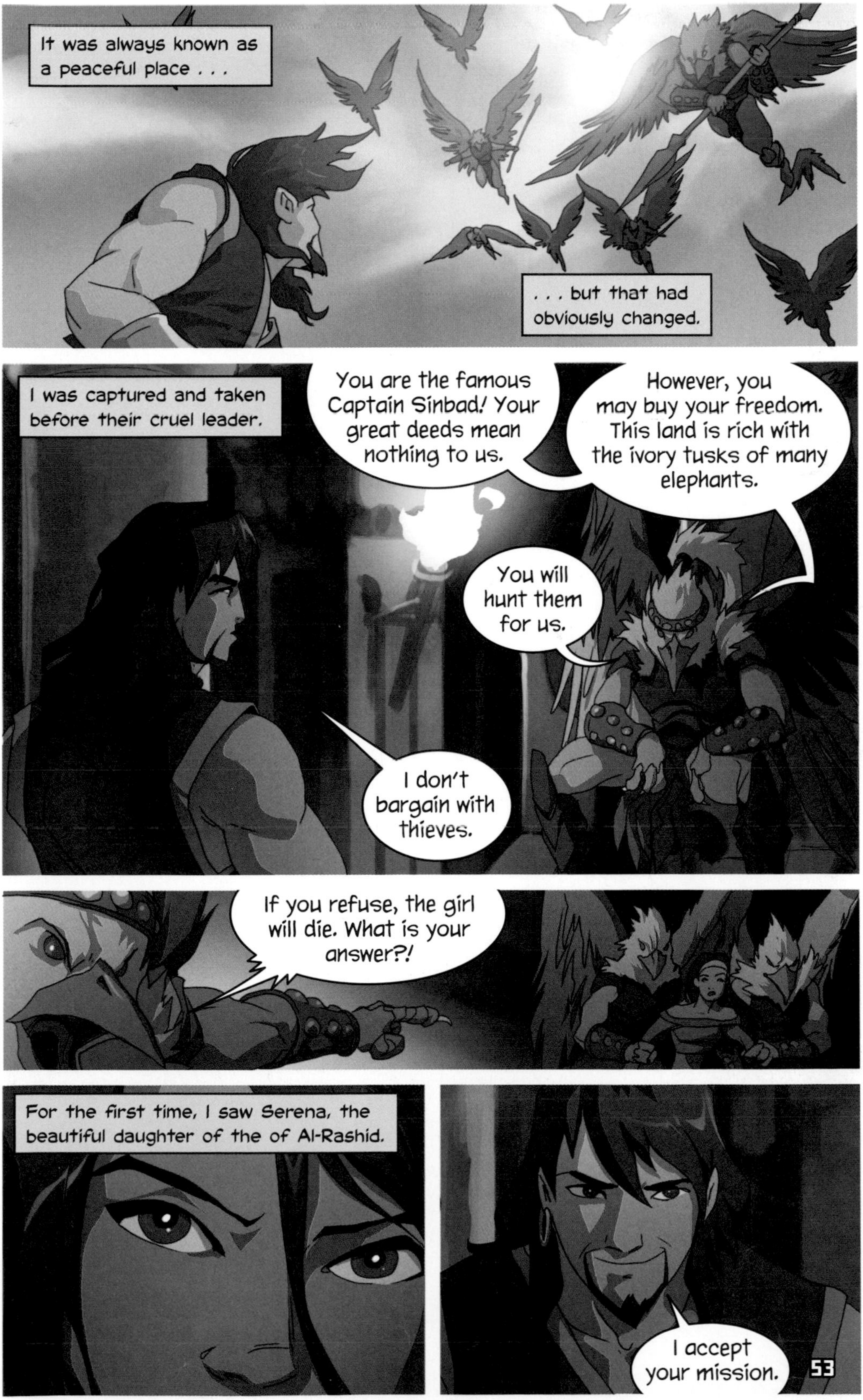
It was always known as a peaceful place . . .
. . . but that had obviously changed.
I was captured and taken before their cruel leader.
You are the famous Captain Sinbad! Your great deeds mean nothing to us.
However, you may buy your freedom. This land is rich with the ivory tusks of many elephants.
You will hunt them for us.
I don't bargain with thieves.
If you refuse, the girl will die. What is your answer?!
For the first time, I saw Serena, the beautiful daughter of the of Al-Rashid.
I accept your mission.

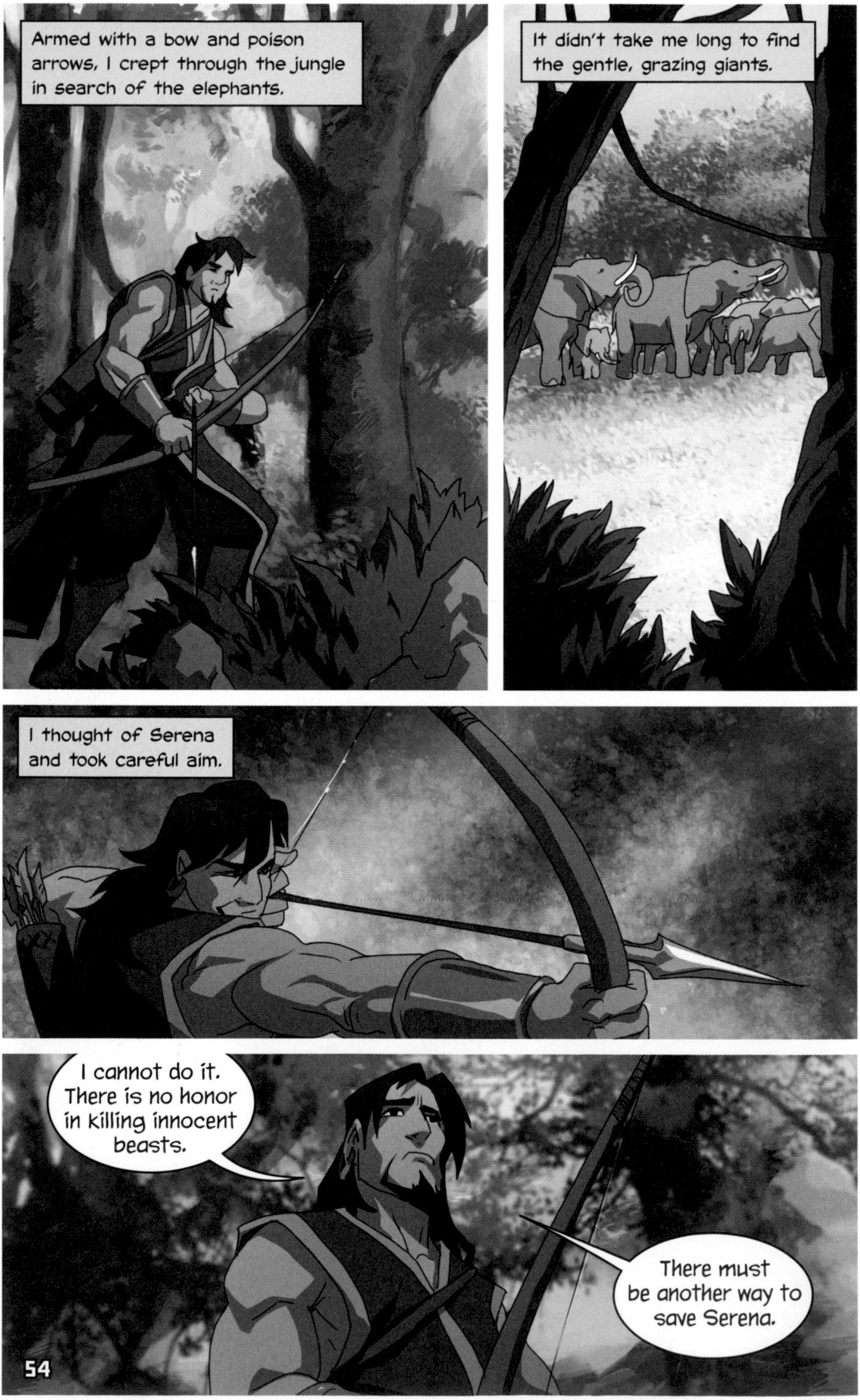
Armed with a bow and poison arrows, I crept through the jungle in search of the elephants.
It didn't take me long to find the gentle, grazing giants.
I thought of Serena and took careful aim.
I cannot do it. There is no honor in killing innocent beasts.
There must be another way to save Serena.

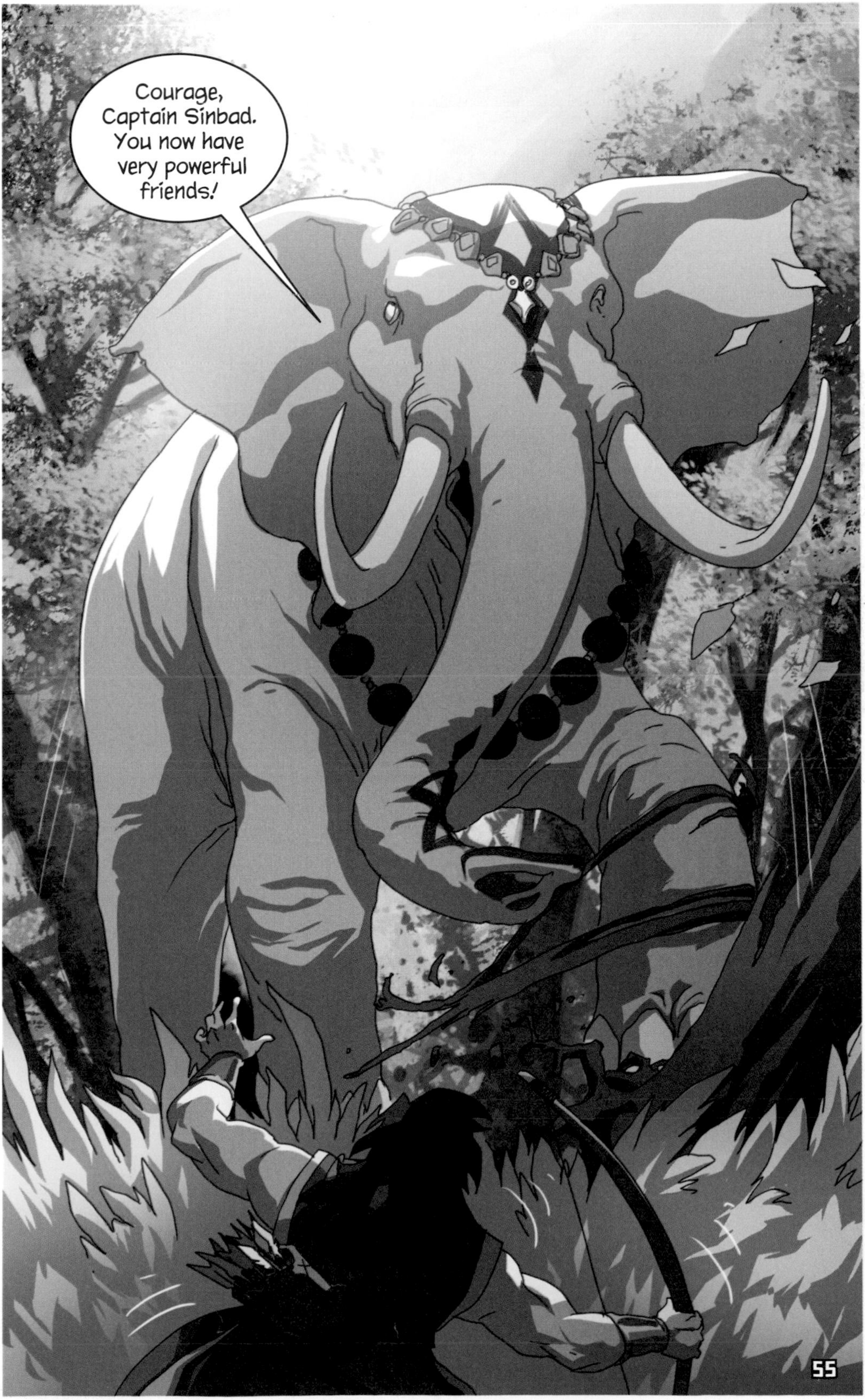
Courage, Captain Sinbad. You now have very powerful friends!

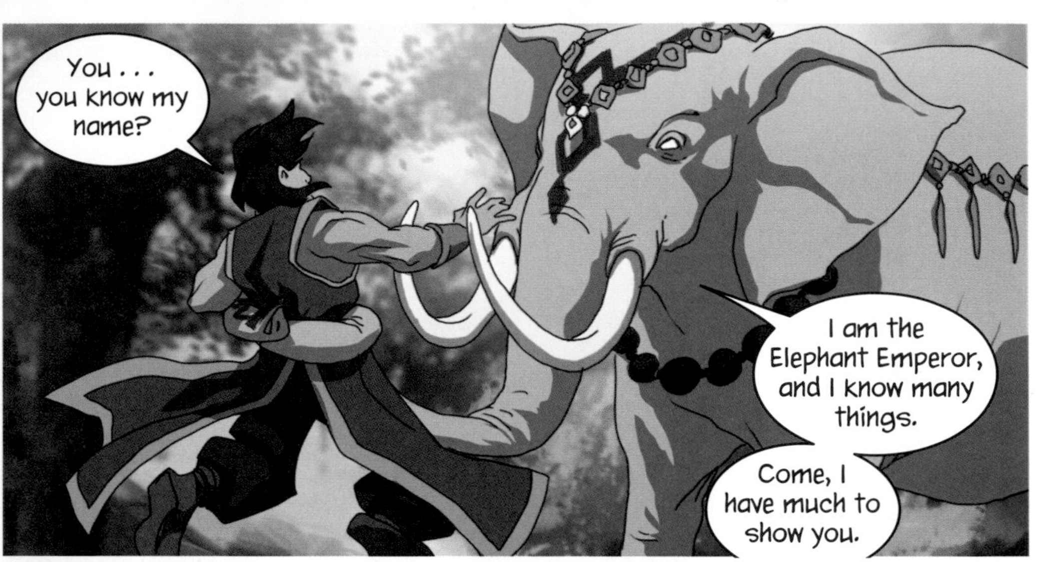
You . . .
you know my
name?
I am the
Elephant Emperor,
and I know many
things.
Come, I
have much to
show you.
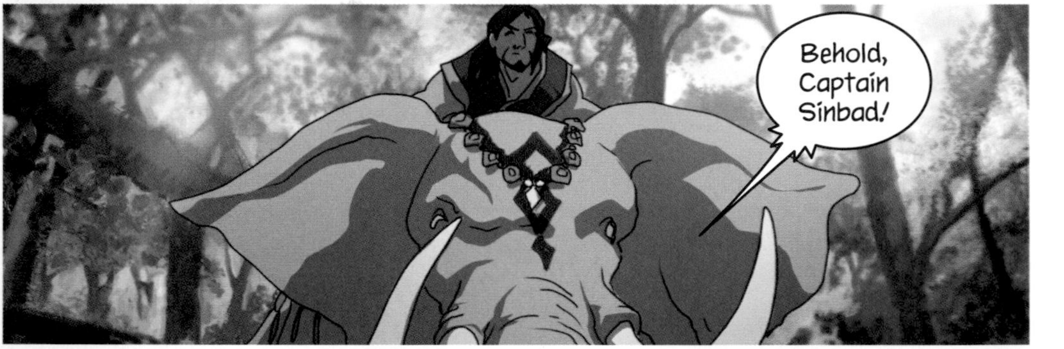
Behold,
Captain
Sinbad!
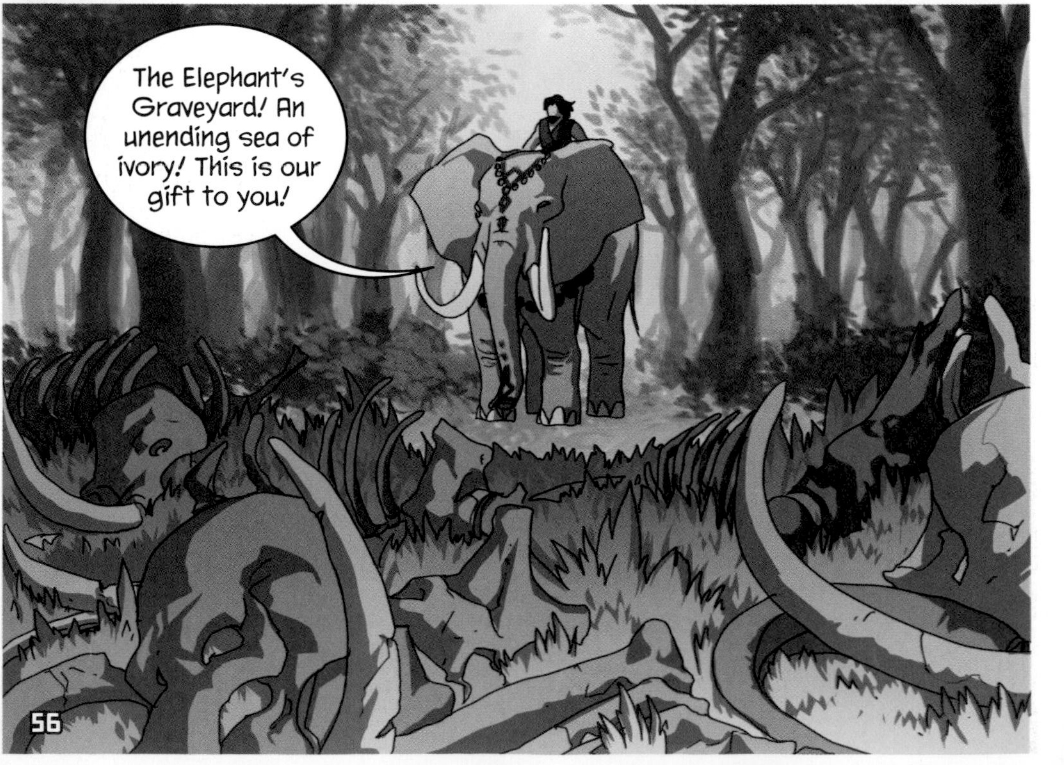
The Elephant's
Graveyard! An
unending sea of
ivory! This is our
gift to you!

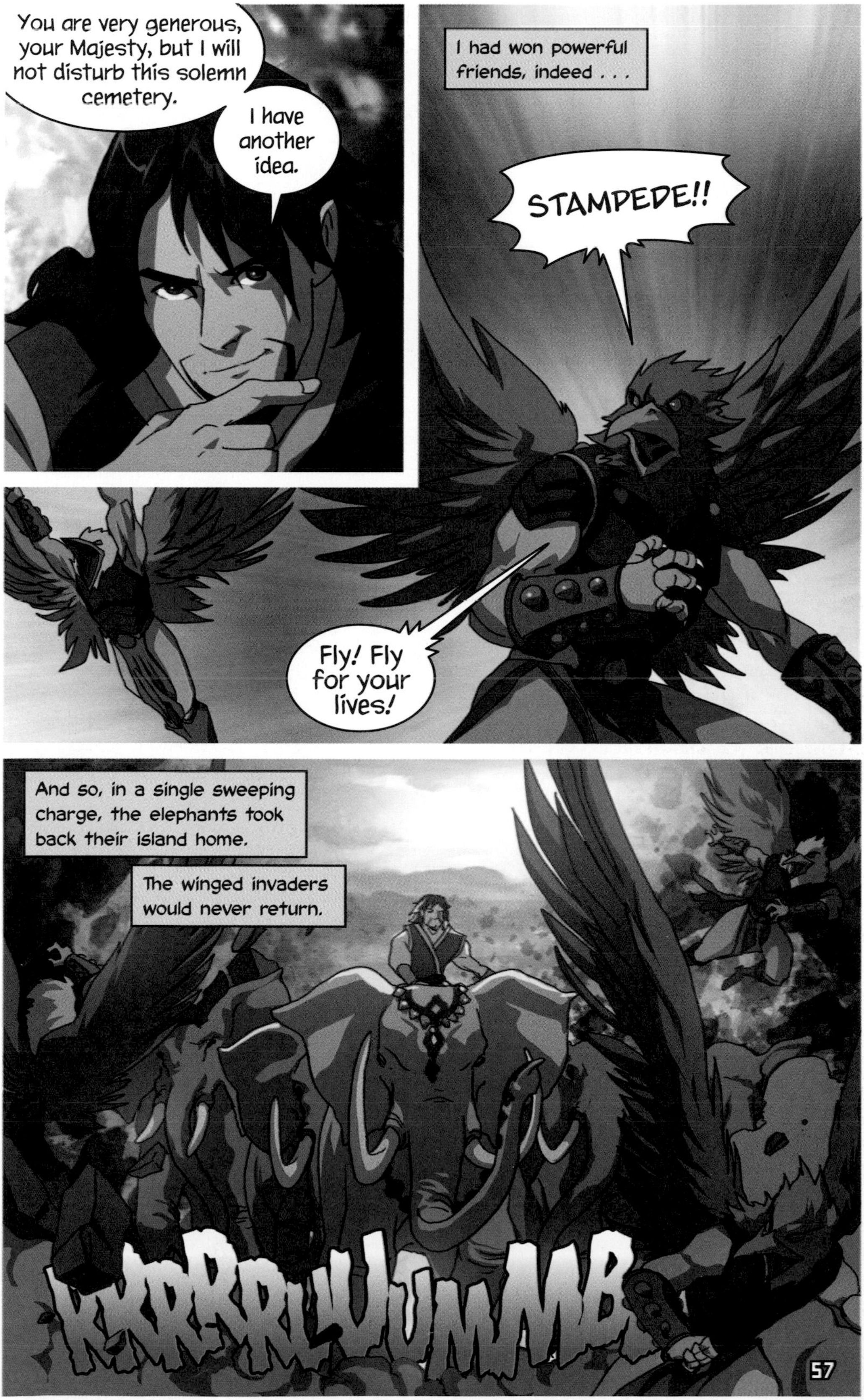
You are very generous, your Majesty, but I will not disturb this solemn cemetery.
I have another idea.
I had won powerful friends, indeed . . .
STAMPEDE!!
Fly! Fly for your lives!
And so, in a single sweeping charge, the elephants took back their island home.
The winged invaders would never return.
KKRRRLUUUMMB

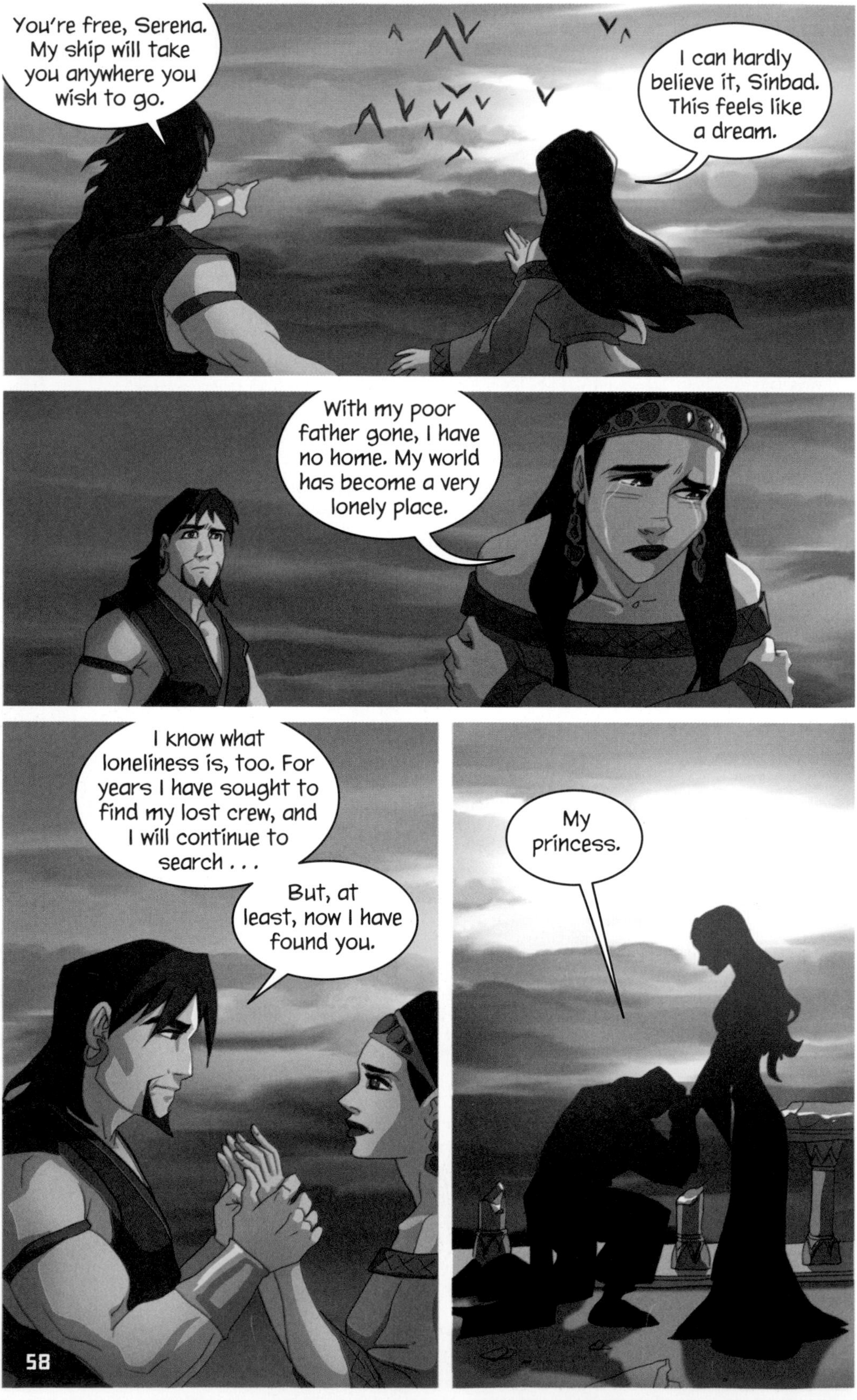
You're free, Serena. My ship will take you anywhere you wish to go.
I can hardly believe it, Sinbad. This feels like a dream.
With my poor father gone, I have no home. My world has become a very lonely place.
I know what loneliness is, too. For years I have sought to find my lost crew, and I will continue to search . . .
But, at least, now I have found you.
My princess.

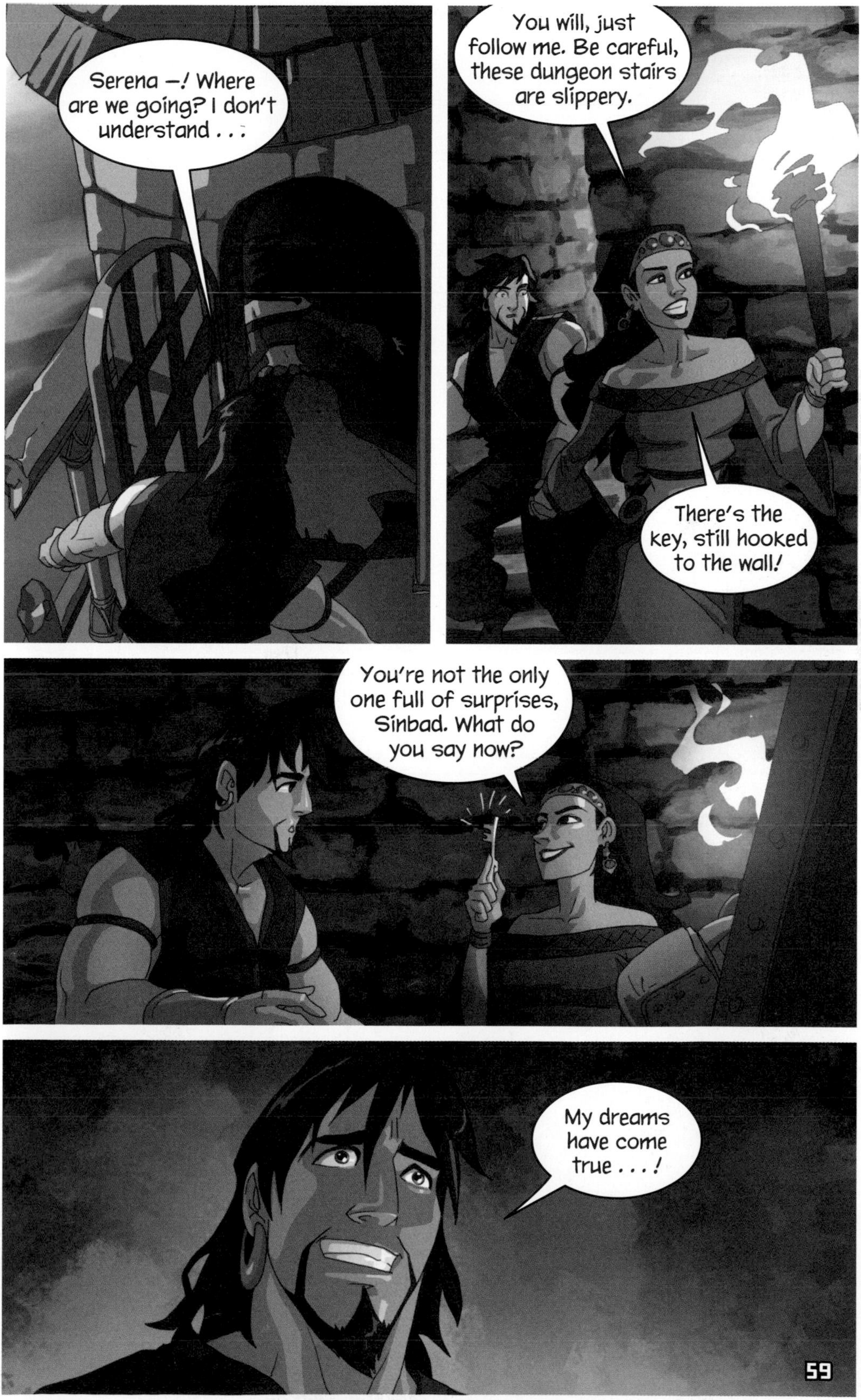
Serena —! Where are we going? I don't understand . . .
You will, just follow me. Be careful, these dungeon stairs are slippery.
There's the key, still hooked to the wall!
You're not the only one full of surprises, Sinbad. What do you say now?
My dreams have come true . . . !

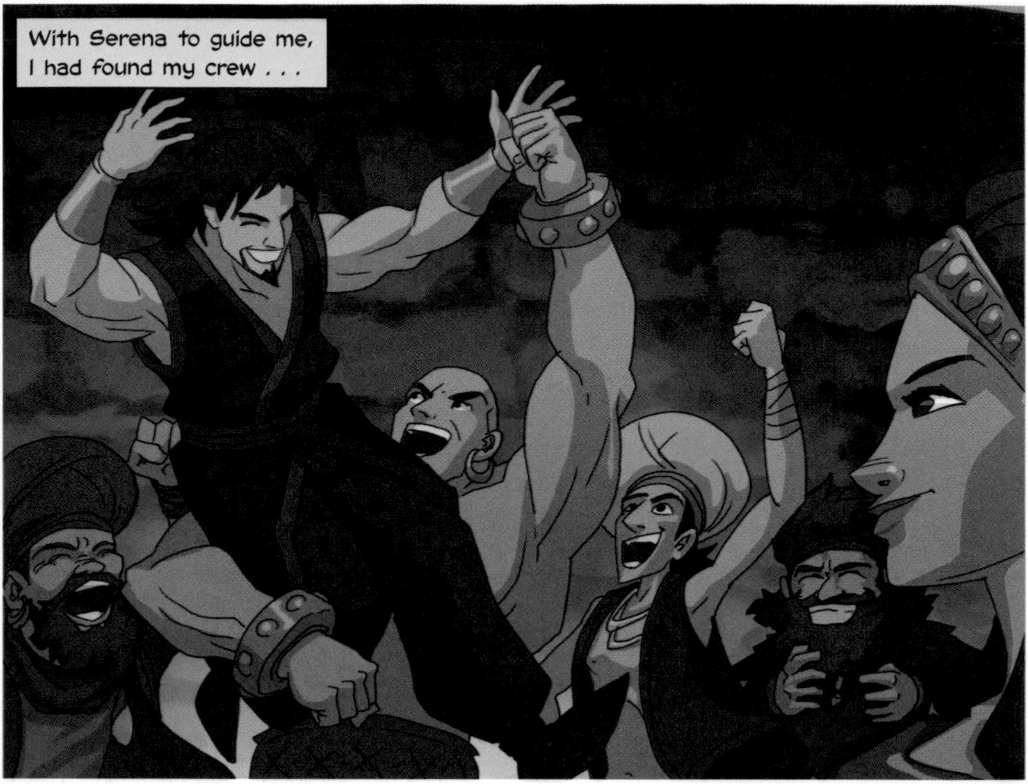
With Serena to guide me,
I had found my crew . . .

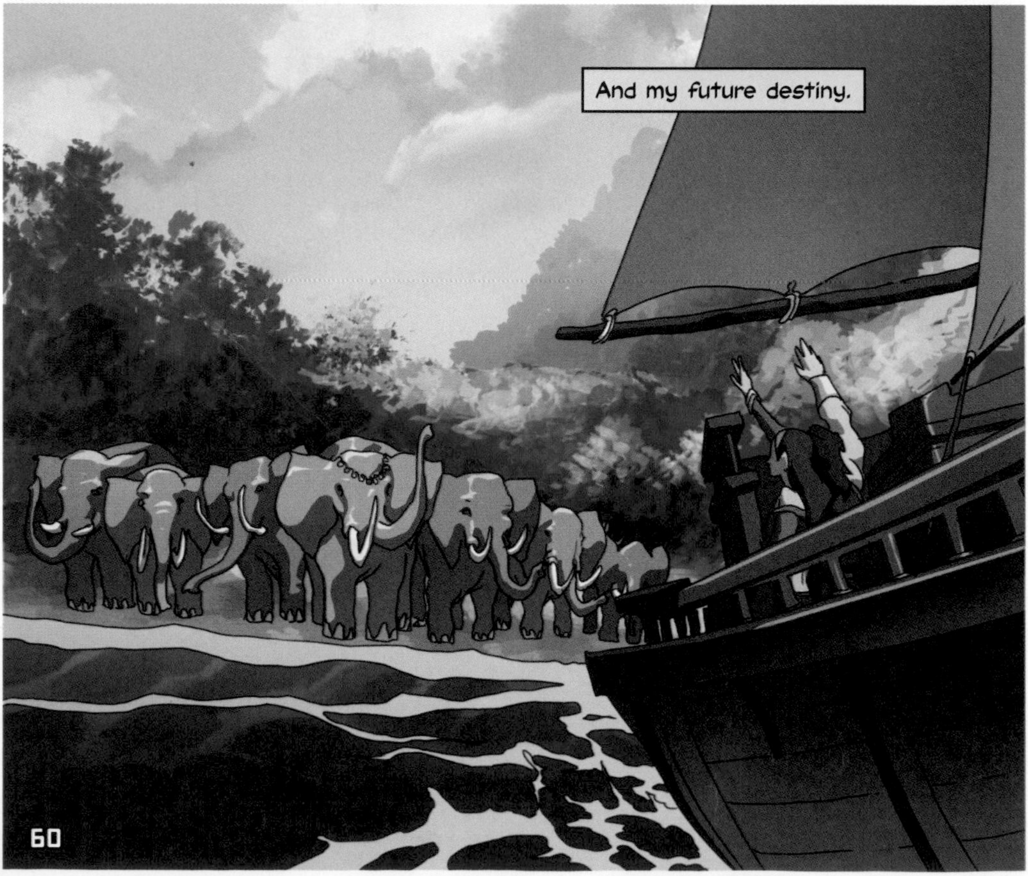
And my future destiny.

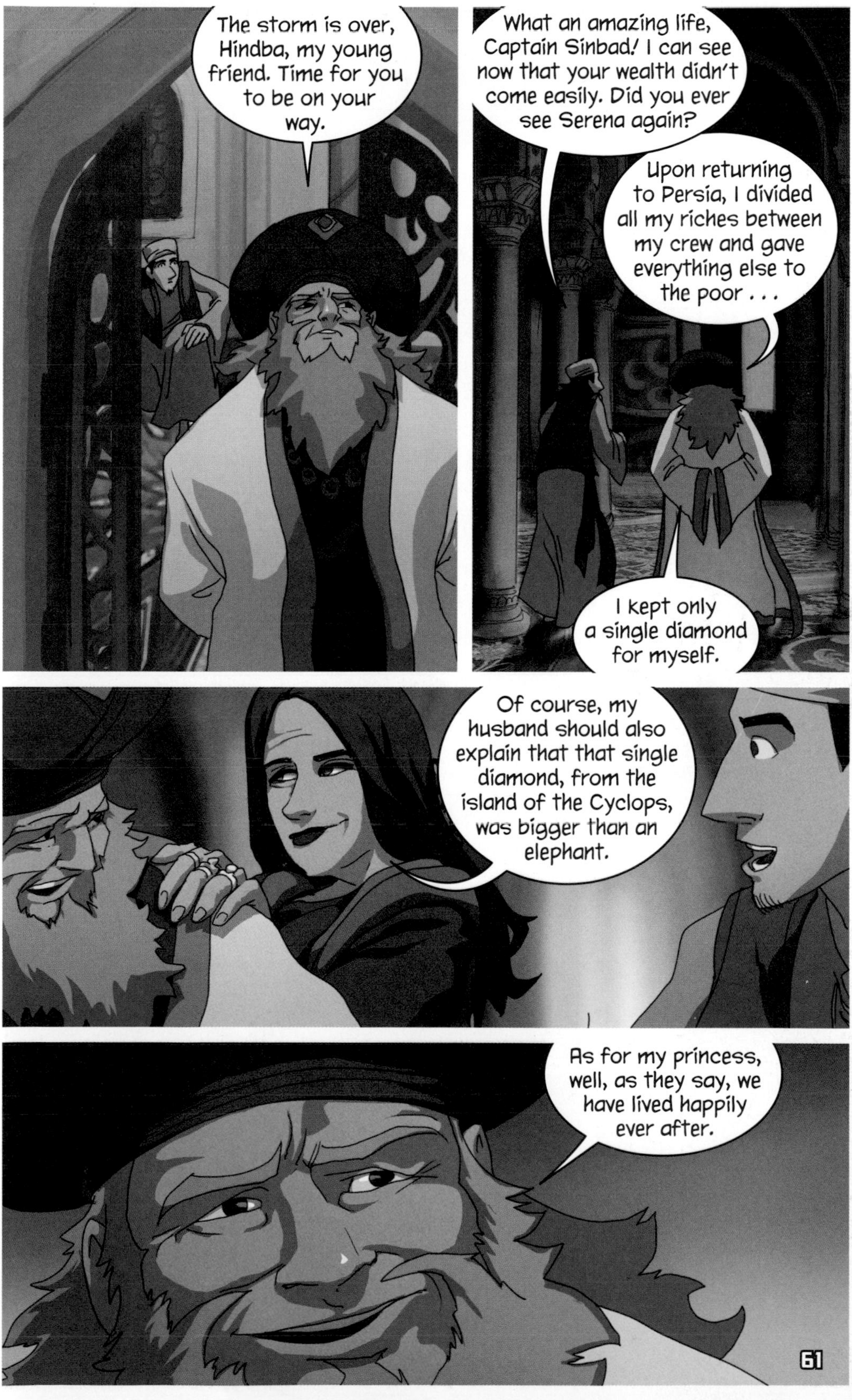
The storm is over, Hindba, my young friend. Time for you to be on your way.
What an amazing life, Captain Sinbad! I can see now that your wealth didn't come easily. Did you ever see Serena again?
Upon returning to Persia, I divided all my riches between my crew and gave everything else to the poor . . .
I kept only a single diamond for myself.
Of course, my husband should also explain that that single diamond, from the island of the Cyclops, was bigger than an elephant.
As for my princess, well, as they say, we have lived happily ever after.

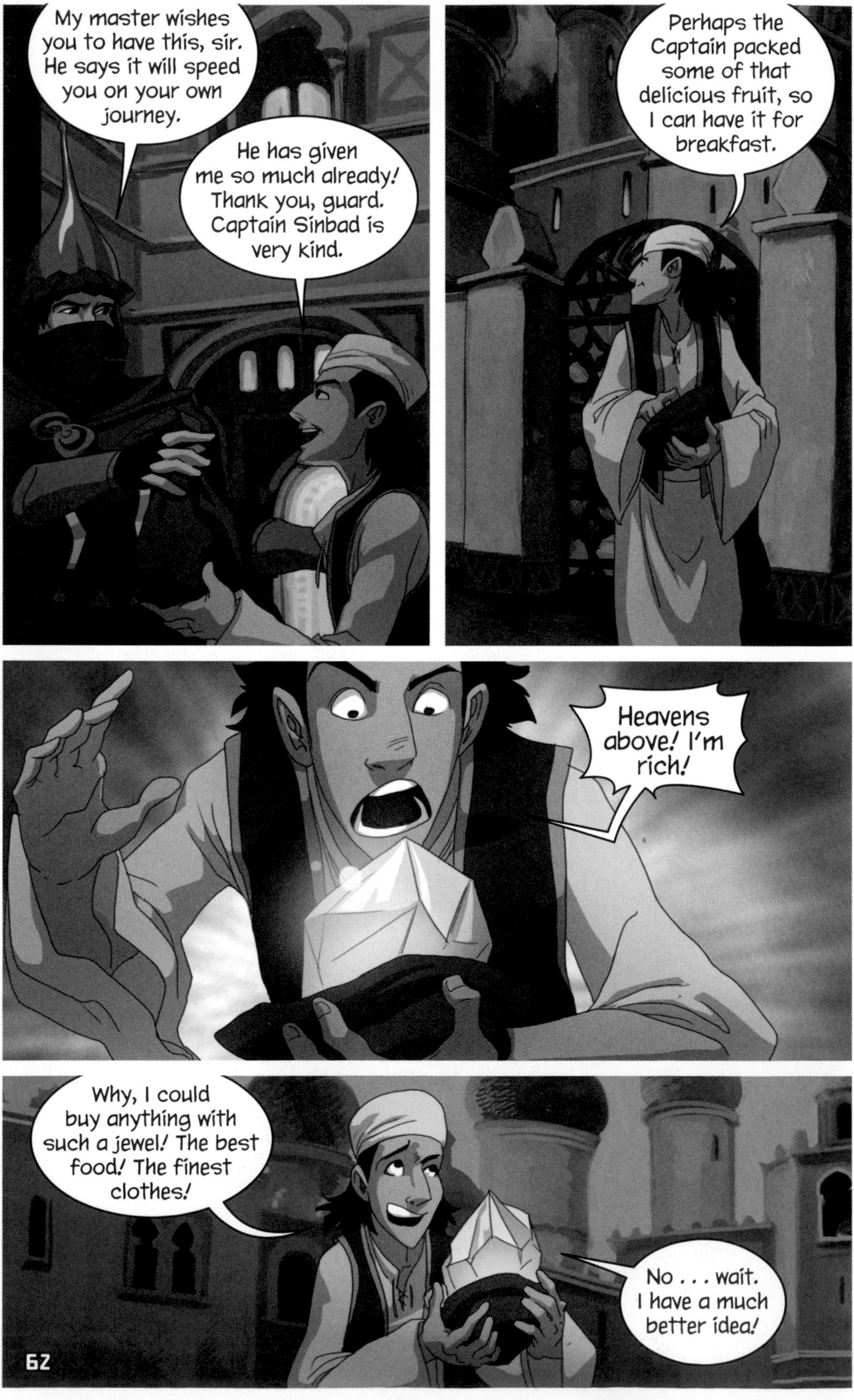
My master wishes you to have this, sir. He says it will speed you on your own journey.
He has given me so much already! Thank you, guard. Captain Sinbad is very kind.
Perhaps the Captain packed some of that delicious fruit, so I can have it for breakfast.
Heavens above! I'm rich!
Why, I could buy anything with such a jewel! The best food! The finest clothes!
No . . . wait. I have a much better idea!

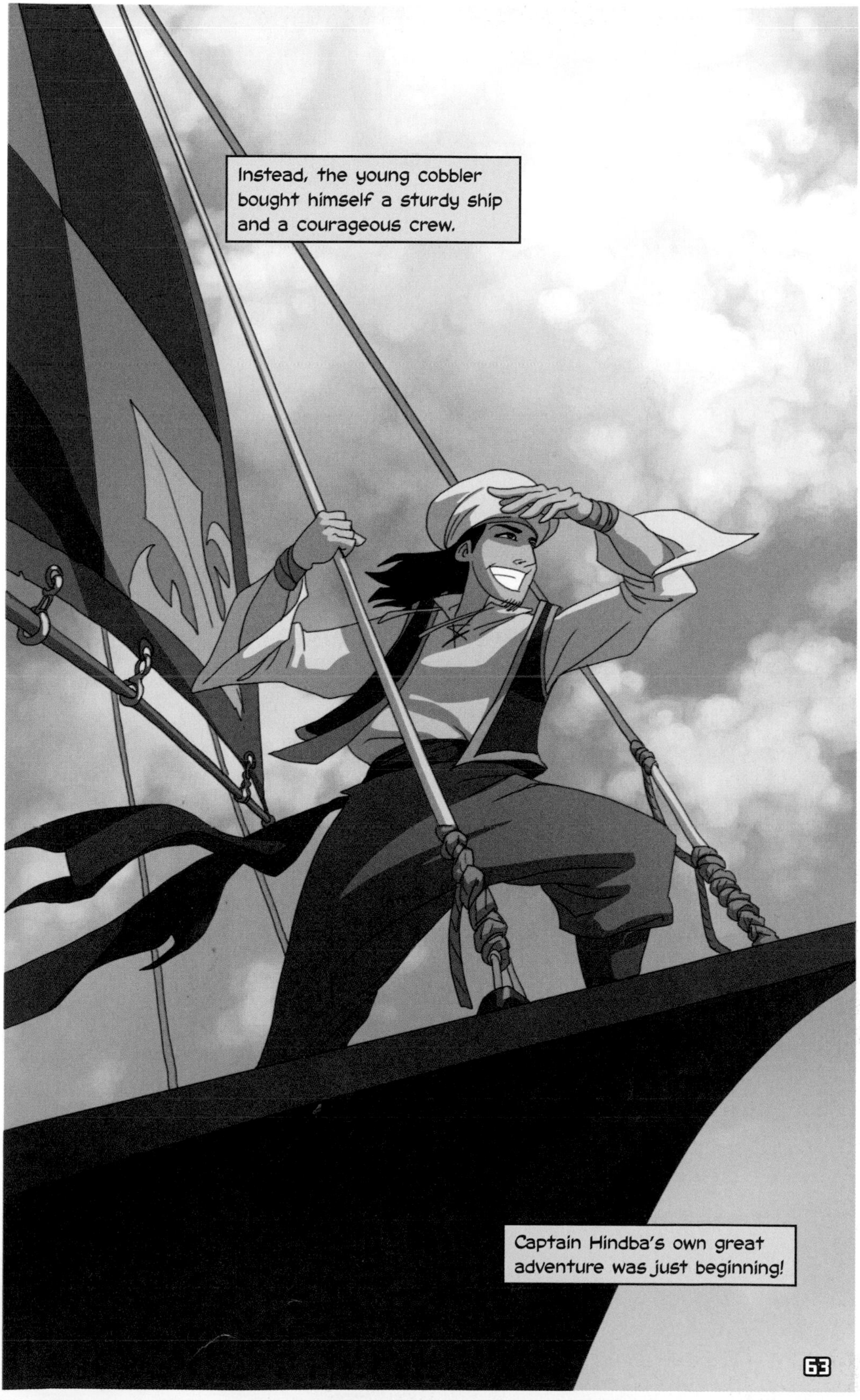
Instead, the young cobbler bought himself a sturdy ship and a courageous crew.
Captain Hindba's own great adventure was just beginning!

ARABIAN NIGHTS

The story of Sinbad the Sailor is part of a collection of Middle Eastern and South Asian folktales known as *One Thousand and One Nights*. These tales have been passed down from generation to generation for hundreds of years. The first English-language edition, titled *The Arabian Nights' Entertainment*, was published in 1706.

Since then, many versions of the book have been published — some containing more than 1,000 stories. In each of these editions, the tales of mystery and adventure are told by the same narrator, a beautiful woman named Scheherazade. She has just married an evil ruler who plans to kill her before the night is through. To stop him, Scheherazade entertains the king with a new story each night, and he soon forgets about his deadly plan.

The Arabian Nights tales remains some of the greatest stories ever told. They include popular adventures, such as "The Fisherman and the Genie," "The Seven Voyages of Sinbad," and "Ali Baba and the Forty Thieves." Many of these stories have been adapted into movies, books, and plays that are still popular today.

REAL-WORLD
EXPLORERS

FERDINAND MAGELLAN

On August 10, 1519, this Spanish sailor left Seville,
Spain, with five ships and a large crew. He returned
three years later, becoming the first explorer to sail
around the world. During the time, Magellan navigated
through the southern strait of South America, which
connects the Alantic and Pacific Oceans. It is now
called the Strait of Magellan.

JUAN PONCE DE LEÓN

In the early 1500s, many believe this
explorer set out from Spain in search of
the Fountain of Youth. Although he didn't
succeed, Ponce de León became the first
European to visit what would become
America, setting foot on Florida in 1513.

ROBERT EDWIN PEARY

On July 6, 1908, this Pennsylvania
man left New York City with
one goal — to reach the
North Pole. Nearly one year
later, he became the first
man to accomplish this
grueling feat.

AUTHOR

Since 1986, Martin Powell has been a freelance writer. He has written hundreds of stories, many of which have been published by Disney, Marvel, Tekno comic, Moonstone Books, and others. In 1989, Powell received an Eisner Award nomination for his graphic novel *Scarlet in Gaslight*. This award is one of the highest comic book honors.

ABOUT THE ILLUSTRATOR

Ferran was born in Monterrey, Mexico, in 1977. For more than a decade, Ferran has worked as a colorist and an illustrator for comic book publishers such as Marvel, Image, and Dark Horse. He currently works for Protobunker Studio while also developing his first graphic novel.

GLOSSARY

ancient *(AYN-shuhnt)*—very old

beggar *(BEG-guhr)*—someone who asks for money or help on the street

cannibal *(KAN-uh-buhl)*—someone who eats human flesh

cursed *(KURSSD)*—under an evil spell

cyclops *(SYE-klahps)*—a monster with a single eye in the middle of its forehead

desolate *(DESS-uh-luht)*—deserted or uninhabited

fiend *(FEEND)*—an evil or cruel person

hypnotized *(HIP-nuh-tized)*—placed someone into a trance

legend *(lej-uhnd)*—a story handed down from earlier times, which is often based on facts but not entirely true

lurking *(LURK-ing)*—moving stealthily to avoid being seen

marooned *(muh-ROOND)*—stuck on a deserted island and unable to leave

merchant *(MUR-chuhnt)*—ships that carry goods for trade

monsoon *(mon-SOON)*—a very strong wind that blows across the Indian Ocean and southern Asia

tempest *(TEM-pist)*—a violent storm or uproar

DISCUSSION QUESTIONS

1. At the end of the story, why do you think Sinbad gave the beggar a large diamond? How did Sinbad hope he would spend it? Explain.

2. Sinbad the Sailor had seven exciting adventures at sea. Which voyage do you think was the most exciting? Explain your answer.

3. Each page of a graphic novel is made up of several illustrations called panels. Which panel of art was your favorite? Why?

WRITING PROMPTS

1. Keep a journal of your own explorations. Write about the places you've been and the adventures you've had.

2. Sinbad had seven voyages. Pretend you're the author and imagine an eighth adventure. Where will the explorer go next? What types of creatures will he face? You decide.

3. Imagine your own Arabian Nights tale. Think of a story filled with mystery and adventure. Then write it down and read it to friends and family.

STONE ARCH BOOKS

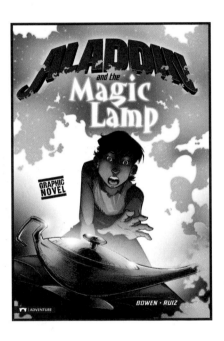

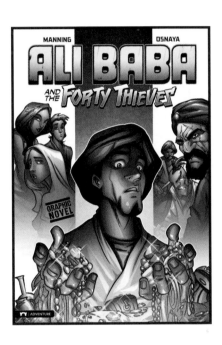

ALADDIN
and the
Magic
Lamp
GRAPHIC NOVEL
ADVENTURE
BOWEN · RUIZ

ALADDIN AND THE MAGIC LAMP

The legendary tale of Aladdin, a poor youth living in the city of Al Kal'as. One day, the crafty boy outsmarts an evil sorcerer, getting his hands on a magical lamp that houses a wish-fulfilling genie! Soon, all of Aladdin's dreams come true, and he finds himself married to a beautiful princess. All is well until, one day, the evil sorcerer returns to reclaim the lamp.

MANNING
OSNAYA
ALI BABA
AND THE FORTY THIEVES
GRAPHIC NOVEL
ADVENTURE

ALI BABA AND THE FORTY THIEVES

The legendary tale of Ali Baba, a young Persian boy who discovers a cave filled with gold and jewels, the hidden treasures of forty deadly thieves. Unfortunately, his greedy brother, Kassim, cannot wait to get his hands on the riches. Returning to the cave, he is captured by the thieves and killed, and now the evil men want revenge on Ali Baba as well.

ARABIAN NIGHTS TALES

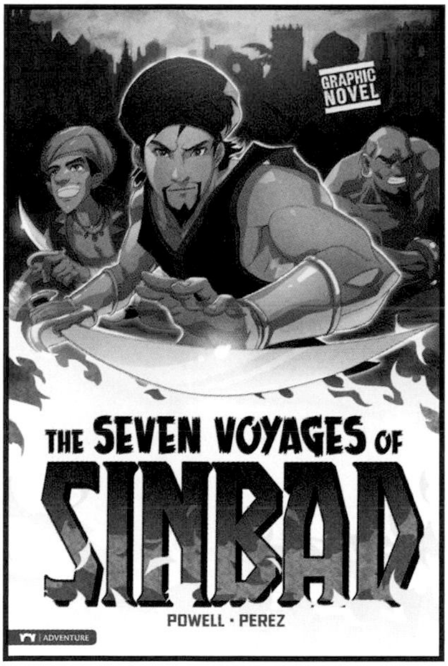
GRAPHIC NOVEL
THE SEVEN VOYAGES OF
SINBAD
POWELL · PEREZ
ADVENTURE

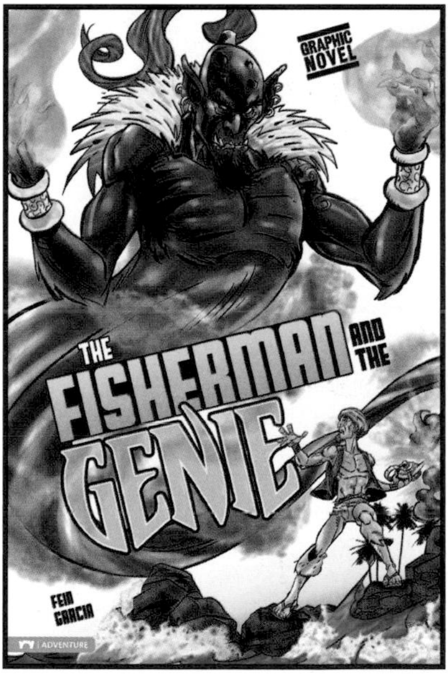
GRAPHIC NOVEL
THE FISHERMAN AND THE GENIE
FEIN
GARCIA
ADVENTURE

THE SEVEN VOYAGES OF SINBAD

The tale of Sinbad the Sailor, who goes to sea in search of great riches and discovers even greater adventures. On his seven treacherous voyages, the Persian explorer braves a shipwreck, fights off savage cannibals, and battles a giant Cyclops, hoping to survive and tell his legendary story.

THE FISHERMAN AND THE GENIE

The legendary tale of an evil Persian king, who marries a new wife each day and then kills her the next morning. To stop this murderous ruler, a brave woman named Scheherazade risks her own life and marries the king herself . . . but not without a plan. On their wedding night, she will entertain him with the tale of the Fisherman and the Genie — a story so amazing, he'll never want it to end.

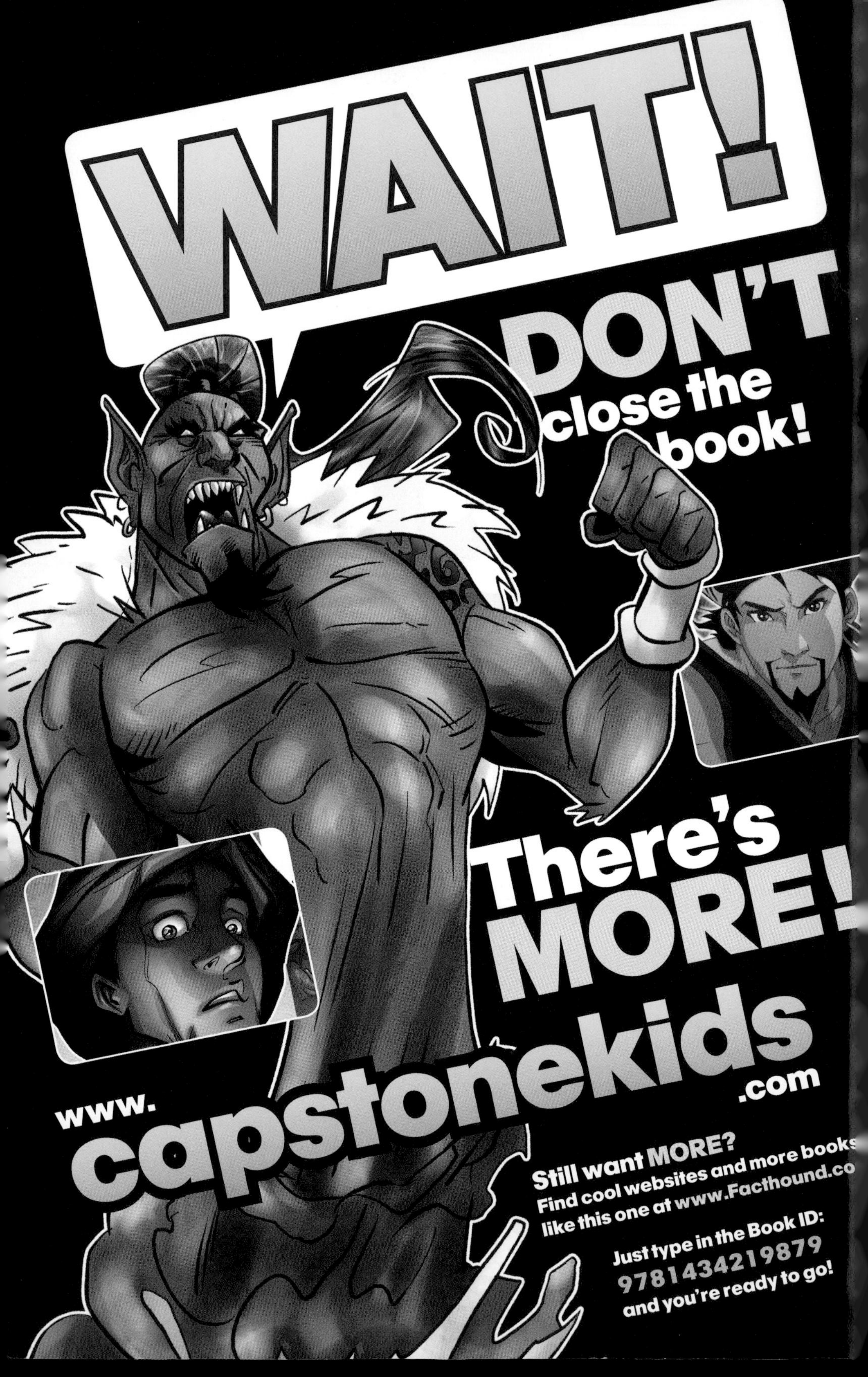
WAIT!
DON'T close the book!
There's MORE!
www.capstonekids.com
Still want MORE?
Find cool websites and more books
like this one at www.Facthound.co
Just type in the Book ID:
9781434219879
and you're ready to go!